HE DID
THEY SAID
GOD IS

(TRUSTING THE PROCESS)

Toni Dyson

He Did. They Said. God Is.

Dedication

In loving memory of my Auntie Doris...

Whenever I was discouraged and wanted to give up during the season of writing my book, my aunt's words of encouragement stuck with me.

"Toniesha, I love your spirit, insight, positive demeanor, and overall outlook on life no matter the situation. Each time you speak out, it shows your wisdom and love for God. You are an amazing individual and a great role model to your cousins and your generation to follow. You are on the right road. Things may change. Don't rush it. With everything you endure in life, please use a pen and paper. It will take you a long way. Write it down, keep loving God the way that you do, and you will win."

I never shared this message with anyone. I kept my auntie's kind words within me. When times were difficult for me, and I couldn't remember her words, I would go to her message to read her words and remind myself of her encouragement. Thank you so much, Aunt D. When I felt alone, misunderstood, not supported, not good enough, or whatever challenges that came my way, your words reminded me to keep going. You may not be here to see the birth of my creation, but I celebrate this moment with you in spirit. I love you always.

Rest Peacefully.

Acknowledgments

It is a genuine pleasure to express my gratitude to God. He has been my source and allowed every page to move and be written around Him. He helped me in every trial and error of these pages as well as in my life. I would not have been able to fulfill His purpose for me to complete this book without His help.

I also want to give thanks to my loving family and friends who have been my backbone and biggest supporters. Thanks to my past pains, people who turned their backs on me, and people who gave up on me, for it has helped build the woman I am today.

A special thanks to my husband, Dimitri… Without him, this story could not be as successful.

Thank you to my mentors Damika, Betty, and Tressa. You all have emotionally pushed me to be the best me I could be. I found my purpose in this process.

A special thanks to my mentor and friend Donna Christopher. We share a true divine connection that I am beyond blessed to receive. You are an author who didn't hold back from teaching me. You have mentored my craft and helped me in the biggest way possible to make this book successful. Furthermore, you have become a great friend! Even when I was crazy enough to doubt my gift, you reminded me and pushed me to know that I would birth this book in due time. These words would never be enough to sum up the emotions I feel behind it. I am forever grateful for you.

I want to express my heartfelt thanks to my editor, Val Pugh-Love. I appreciate you for your guidance along the journey of completing my first book. Thanks so much for helping bring peace to all my worries. I am grateful for your words of encouragement, insight, assistance, and invaluable support. I can't stress this enough. You are truly incredible!

Most of all, thank you to everyone who invested your time and finances into this book.

To all the women who have been a victim of a broken heart, experienced a pretend love that lacks genuine truth in the meaning of love, and searched for true love to fill the emptiness of their hearts to be loved unconditionally as you are, it's time to stop placing the right heart that God blessed you with in the wrong hands.

Introduction

There are so many people in the world that crave to love and to be loved. Some go to the extreme to find love and question what keeps them from finding true love, while others find themselves in unwanted situations that appear to be love but lack the genuineness of what love is. You are about to engage in heartfelt emotional stories that reflect the many different situations that women face when searching for true love. Each of these women tells stories about their journey to find love and the effects that the lack of love imposed on their lives.

These stories are simply pages in the lives of young women who share moments from their love lives to serve a purpose, to teach, to heal, and to help others gain an understanding of their truths and reasoning. You should never judge a page in someone's life without knowing the full story of their entire truth. In most cases, it is always untold. Instead, learn from their stories, see if you can find yourself in similar situations, or admit to your truth if you have indeed experienced similar situations. Then, think about how you will or have overcome.

> **"I am just a young girl with a big dream**
> **who became a woman with a vision."**
> **Author Unknown**

As a woman who may be single, dating, married, separated, or divorced, I strongly believe that you can relate to these stories and can gain guidance or thought-provoking moments that can help you in this season of your life. When it comes to learning and understanding different love languages and what true love means and consists of, know that you are not alone. We all have searched for the true meaning of love at one point or another in our lives. Understand that everyone will go through a good or bad experience searching for love in this lifetime. As much as it may pain you, it is a part of your growth and will help you become a better woman when loving and being loved once you learn from the pains of finding love.

Today, being social has increased through outlets such as social media. People give power to portraying an image of looking as close to perfection as possible. Some people want to appear to be perfect while hiding behind fake smiles and made up words to project a life they wish they had. They strive to look the part of what they consider to be perfect. They pretend to have the perfect job and even the perfect relationship. For this reason, we must not compare ourselves to others. Their journey is their own, and we may never know what it took for them to get to the moments of their right now or what they may struggle with behind closed doors.

Some people live in secret, afraid or ashamed of what people will think of them if they had a glimpse into their reality. Let's be real, we all share common stories of life from some point in which we have lived and experienced similar situations. One of my biggest goals in writing this book is to help you be real with yourself, acknowledge your very own truth, and become a better you in due time. I want you to think about your relationship, think about love, and think about what true love means to you.

I pray that you can gain answers to your situation and learn how to get through any undesired circumstances in your life. I pray that you learn how to overcome the pain you have experienced in past relationships. It is time to learn how to stop placing the right heart that God blessed you with into the wrong hands. I want you always to remember that the right one, the one that God has ordained for your life, that true love spirit, first lives inside of you. I hope you can receive great understanding and insight for your own life, the words written, and the stories being told within these pages. Remember never to lose sight of the true love you should always have for yourself.

As I leave my footprints in the sand for you to learn from and maybe even follow to better your life, I hope that the journey of these women helps you to renew your mind and see things that you may also be experiencing from a different point of view. A renewed mind can help you change the rules that allow access to your heart and set standards in your life so that you may oversee who is allowed into your space. Doing so will prevent a revolving door of love or the lack thereof. We each have endured or will endure lust, love, being in love, and heartbreak during our lives. It was placed upon my heart to share these stories and to equip you with the most powerful secret weapon that can get you through it all.

I challenge you to not only focus on the end of each story but to feel the love and learn from each chapter. Think about your current situation of love. Know that it does not have to be your ending. True love is desired and a part of God's plan for His children. Never give up on love. Continue reading each story, light a candle, grab your favorite coffee mug or wine glass, and enjoy reading each journey of love. Keep an open mind and reflect on their situations. Then, think about your journey of true love.

Chapter 1

How Did the Relationships You've Witnessed Impact Your Relationships?

Proverbs 22:6

"Train up a child in the way he should go; even when he is old he will not depart from it."

"Again? Where is that bumping sound coming from? It's getting louder. What could it possibly be?" Monet thought to herself. She could hear what sounded like a light thumping sound coming from the hallway. It was only loud enough to hear when silence was present. However, the noise wouldn't allow her to close her eyes and sleep. She quietly turned over in bed and faced the direction of the noise to see if she could make out what it was, but it suddenly stopped. Now that she was wide awake, Monet grabbed her phone and called her friend Nichole. She was an amazing friend to Monet and would answer no matter what time it was or how busy she might be. They made each other a priority.

Nichole answered in a whisper, "Hello."

"Hey. What's up, girl? Did I wake you?" Monet asked.

"Hey, Monet. Naw… I'm up. What's going on?"

"Girl, I can't sleep. I can hear noises coming from down the hall. We both know this is not my house, so I don't want to get up and go investigate."

Nichole laughed. "Girl, you fear your own shadow."

They both laughed at her comment. After more brief words, they agreed that it was probably just Monet's mind messing with her.

Monet said, "Okay girl. Go ahead and get some rest."

The noise had stopped, so Monet was going to try to sleep as well. She ended the call and attempted to go to sleep. However, a few moments later, she heard a door shut followed by a small cry. Monet was concerned. She was staying the night at her friend Tia's home. Tia was an only child and lived with her mom. Earlier that day, Monet wanted to spend some quality time with her, and they ended up arranging to sleepover. Monet's mom was overprotective of her, but she felt Tia's house would be safe. Monet had thought about what she would say if her mom declined her request to stay with Tia for the night. What could go wrong? She looked over to see that Tia was still asleep. None of the noises woke her.

She softly asked, "Tia you up?" to be sure she was asleep.

Tia made a disturbed "Hmm" noise. If Monet had to guess what she was moaning, it would be, *"Leave me alone. I'm asleep."* Monet decided to get out of the bed to investigate the sounds. As she cracked the door, the noise became a little louder. Her friend's mom was down the hall crying. Her boyfriend, who no one knew about, had beat her up and told her not to say one word. She was doing what he told her to do and getting help didn't seem to be an option. He wasn't there when they were eating dinner and then watching T.V. into the late hours of the night. So, Monet assumed he came to the house once everyone was in bed.

She could only guess why he wasn't there earlier in the day. Maybe he showed up late because of his lifestyle, or maybe Tia's mom didn't want her to see him. Monet couldn't tell what was going on, but she knew something wasn't right. Tia's mom turned towards the door and noticed it was cracked open. She waited to see who was standing there. When she realized Monet hadn't said anything, she looked up and softly asked her, "You okay?"

Monet quietly said, "Yes."

Tia's mother pretended as if nothing was wrong. She told Monet to go back into the room and assured her that everything was okay. However, Monet knew she was lying. Instead of going back inside the room she said, "I need to use the bathroom."

"Oh okay. Sure. I'm sorry. Go ahead."

As Monet exited the bedroom, she walked extremely slowly towards the bathroom.

Again, Tia's mom asked, "Are you okay?"

Monet wondered how she could be asking her if she was okay when she didn't seem to be okay herself. Even if Monet was okay or not, she felt that she couldn't help Tia's mom at that time.

Monet quickly responded, "Yes," before entering the bathroom.

She stayed in there for a while to see if she could hear anything more. Suddenly, she heard a ringing cell phone. Tia's mom answered in a low voice. Monet assumed it must have been the abusive boyfriend calling because it sounded like she closed the door to her room in an attempt to keep Monet from hearing her conversation. The door she heard shut earlier was the boyfriend leaving the house. Monet couldn't hear the voice on the other end of the phone, but she heard her friend's mom say, "You hurt me, Teddy. This time, you hurt me bad. I can't do this anymore."

The sound of her voice gave the impression that he was apologizing for his actions. Although she was rejecting his apology, it sounded like she wasn't mentally strong enough to leave him alone. This moment was confusing for any girl to witness. The mixed messages she displayed left a negative impression for Monet. She wondered why any woman would allow a man to treat her that way. After witnessing that ordeal, it began to make sense why Tia would act a little strange from time to time. She has extreme anger issues. Tia is the friend that's always ready to pop off on anyone and ask questions later. She never gave any reasons why her attitude came off as hard as it did. She acted as if her behavior was a normal lifestyle.

Monet wanted to ask Tia about what happened, but she didn't feel it was good timing to address her about something so personal especially if she wasn't aware. Monet didn't know if Tia would believe her or think she was lying about the situation. So, she decided to leave it alone for the moment. Had Monet's mother known Tia's mom had those issues going on in her life, she would not have had the opportunity to go to Tia's house. Monet would usually tell her mother everything, but if she told her what happened only a few feet away from her, Monet's mom would have a fit. She thought it would be best to leave out that part of the night.

Monet went home early the next morning to get ready for school. Her alarm went off at 5:15 a.m. as she was walking into her home. The night skies were slowly fading as the sun started to pierce the sky. Monet put on black leggings and a blue hoodie. She laced up her New Balance shoes and prepared her playlist before hitting the streets of Maryland for an early morning run. She preferred to run in the early part of the morning, so she could get back home to shower before school.

After her morning run, she washed the sweat from her body and dressed for class. She rode the bus to school. That morning she found herself sitting in a window seat gazing at people standing along the sidewalk as the bus passed them. She was deep in thought about what she wanted to do in life. People often told her she was just a young girl and should only focus on finishing school. However, her mind wouldn't accept what others wanted her to do. Instead, she constantly desired to do more with her life. Something unique about her made her stand out from others.

As the bus ride continued, she put her headphones in her ears, pressed play, and listened to a phenomenal motivational speaker from her playlist. His voice echoed in her ears, *"Keep running the race. Don't give up! Don't become small-minded. Change your circle and push toward success."* She was encouraged tremendously.

When the bus arrived at school, Monet exited and headed towards the cafeteria to meet her girls before class. Ariel, Monet's best friend, asked if all the girls would like to come over to her home after school to hang out. Monet, Saniya, and Tia all agreed to meet. Michelle and Nichole said they had after-school practice for the fashion show and could not join them.

At 2:45 p.m., the last bell rang. Monet and Tia were in the same class, so they left class together and searched for Saniya and Ariel. They would get on the bus together and head to Ariel's house. Before they could find the girls, they received a group text message from Ariel saying, "Bus Lot 309." It took Saniya longer than everyone else to get there. She never rode the bus because she lived close enough to the school to be considered a walker. Although the bus ride was new to her, being surrounded by her girls was fun. They all took selfies, laughed, and engaged in small talk. They went back and forth debating if they should order pizza or carry-out when the bus driver suddenly stopped the bus and parked it.

He turned around and angrily asked, "Who threw the paper?"

No one answered, so the bus driver told everyone he was turning the bus around to head back to school if no one confessed.

Unsurprisingly, there was more silence.

Saniya said, "What the hell? I should've gone home."

Her first experience riding the school bus was becoming a regretful one. All the girls were closer to home than they were to the school and didn't want to ruin their afternoon on the bus. As the bus driver started to say, "I'm turning the bus aro-," seven people at the back of the bus stood up, grabbed their things, and got off the bus. As they got off, they yelled out they would walk the rest of the way to their homes. Everyone knew that it was one of them that threw the paper, so the driver continued taking everyone else home.

As the girl's walked down the hill towards Ariel's place, they agreed pizza would be easier. Anthony, Ariel's boyfriend, walked up behind them. Monet already knew him from previous encounters, so she hugged him. Ariel introduced the other girls as they stood a few feet away so that the couple could talk privately. Marcellus, Anthony's friend, came towards the crew smiling because he thought he had a shot with one of them. However, no one was interested in giving him any of their time.

Anthony wrapped up his conversation with Ariel when they arrived at her home. He told her that he and Marcellus were headed to the store. Ariel asked which one. He told her he was going to the 7/11 at the top of the hill. She asked him to pick up their pizza instead of calling for delivery and having to pay a delivery fee. He agreed, and Ariel went upstairs to retrieve twenty dollars for their pizza. She knew the other girls were splitting the cost with her and would be giving her money back.

As they waited for their pizza, they sat around joking, gossiping, and browsing social media. The time was passing quickly. Anthony had yet to come back, and he wasn't answering his cell phone. The girls were upset that he had not made it back with their food to satisfy their starving bellies. He had their money, so going out themselves was not an option. While they continued to wait, Saniya informed Monet that someone in school was crushing on her. Monet was far from interested in dating. She had a big heart and loved hard, and knew she needed to protect it. Saniya was saying how cool he was, and of course, that led Monet to ask who the mystery guy was.

"Wendell!" Saniya said.

Monet replied with curiosity in her voice, Wendell? Wendell, the boxer?"

"Yes," Saniya said.

Monet thought he was very unattractive. She said, "I'm okay. I'll pass."

The night slowly came to an end, and the girls' parents came to pick them up. Anthony never came back with the money or their pizza. They were disturbed feeling as if he had stolen from them. The next day at the fashion show, Monet pulled Ariel aside and asked, "Have you spoken to your boyfriend?"

"No, I haven't heard from him at all," Ariel said.

"Should we be worried? I mean, surely he wouldn't have just taken the money," Monet asked Ariel with a concerned look on her face.

They weren't sure if they should be worried about his safety or if he deliberately took the money with no intentions of coming back.

"I don't know what happened or what to think, but I am worried a bit," Ariel responded.

She was embarrassed that he didn't come back, but she was also worried that something bad might have happened to him. Monet could tell that she was bothered by the situation, so she decided to change the subject.

"I'm sure he is okay and has a good explanation. Let's go watch this show get your mind off him."

They all went to support their girls Michelle and Nichole. Since they couldn't hang out the night before because of practice for the fashion show, this was just another way for them to spend time together and support each other at the same time. The show progressed, and the models looked stunning. Wendell walked out looking like a new young man. He looked nice all dressed up for the show. He caught Monet's eye. She couldn't take her eyes off him as he moved smoothly down the runway. She whispered to Saniya, "I think I want to take back what I said yesterday."

They both laughed and continued to watch the show. Afterward, Saniya connected Wendell and Monet. As time went on, they became more than friends. They had an immature but loving relationship. Part of the reason Monet initially turned Wendell down was because of the things she'd heard about him. Thinking about the stories she heard about him and how he was with her led her to wonder why everyone thought he was so mean, rude, and disrespectful. She didn't want to waste any time taking chances on love, especially when people had already warned her. However, she didn't see what everyone said about him. After talking and getting to know each other, she came to her conclusion that he was loving and very charming. When she described him to her friends, she would say, "He is very intelligent and soft as a teddy bear."

Monet had been going through a lot mentally. She was stressing about friendships, her relationship, school, and just life itself. She had mood swings, and everything seemed to irritate her. Monet arrived home that evening and asked her mom for some assistance. Because her mom didn't respond to her request immediately, Monet reverted to her spoiled ways. They had different views and disagreed on a lot, but they could still talk and laugh with each other as if nothing happened. Monet was upset at this point because she felt that she and her needs were not a priority for her mom.

Monet was on the phone with Wendell when she and her mom were at odds. As she ended the conversation with her mom, Wendell told her she was so lucky to have the kind of parents she had. At that moment, she didn't want to hear comments about how lucky she was to have her parents. She didn't understand why anyone would say she was lucky after engaging in a disagreement. She wanted to scream, holler, and turn her anger towards him, but she knew that would be wrong. He didn't do anything to her. She took a deep breath, brushed it off, and ended their conversation shortly after that. Monet spoke to

Wendell again later that night, but this time he was the one upset.

"Yo, I hate my life! God could take it now!"

Monet is a lover. Her heart was so heavy after hearing him say those words. It hurt her more than anything to be a witness of someone saying something so cruel. Nevertheless, she realized she was not the only one with problems. Just like others got through their trials, she could, too. God wouldn't allow her to look at the bad in Wendell. Instead, she understood his behavior. So, she dug deeper into the reason he felt that way. She wanted to understand how and why he developed so much anger.

The next day around noon, she was on her way to the mall to grab a few items for her trip with her family. While she was shopping, Wendell called and asked her so many questions.

"Where are you? How long will you be there? Who are you with?"

She got tired of answering all of his questions and asked him, "Why? What's wrong, Wendell?"

He replied, "I'm about to come by. I need to talk."

He was direct and wanted to see her face to face instead of talking on the phone. She didn't have a chance to object, so she waited for him to arrive. She saw him coming from a mile away and instantly got excited.

She yelled, "Heeeeyyyyyyy, Butt-Butt!"

He hated when she called him that. When she got closer to him, she noticed that he looked upset. She knew he didn't like the name, but she had never seen him react with the look he was giving her at that moment. She looked closer and noticed he had been crying and had bruises all over his face. She momentarily stood in shock before quickly rushing towards him. She hugged him and tried to relieve his pain. Instead, she was hurting him with her touch. "Ahhh," he winced out in pain.

She backed up from him and could see that he had bruises on his back, too. A million questions ran through her mind, but she couldn't put them into words. This moment was sad for them both. Seeing him in that condition left her speechless. She hesitated for a moment but decided to ask him one question, "Who did this to you?"

As they sat and talked about what happened, she started to understand why he said she was lucky to have parents like hers. He proceeded to tell her about how his father was abusive to his mom. This day, Wendell got in the way of the abuse. Monet was in shock as she listened to him tell the story of what happened. As he watched the abuse, his Dad told him to go to his room. With tears filling his eyes, he softly asked his dad to stop hitting his mother.

"Dad, can you stop?" he recalled through tears.

As his dad struck her again, he looked over at Wendell and angrily said, "What!?"

With fear in his voice, but bravery in his heart Wendell said a little louder, "Can you stop hitting my mom? She's hurt."

Wendell said he could see the anger in his father's eyes. He told Wendell to shut up then turned his anger towards him and began to beat him, too. He left visible bruises and scars on both Wendell and his mother. Monet had a heavy heart about what happened. She decided to tread lightly with Wendell. Sometimes his behavior was a lot to deal with, but she now knew he was hurting and why. She finally understood why he would be angry with everyone for no real reason. If things didn't go his way, he wanted to fight. Wendell used to box for sport. Therefore, he knew that with his big muscles and his strength, people automatically feared having a confrontation with him. If anyone ever made Monet feel unsafe or tried to harm her in any way, he went into defense mode in a matter of seconds, filling the perpetrator with fear and regret.

After that day of revelation, Monet and Wendell continued dating. Two years later, Monet realized that Wendell was still holding on to his past pain. She repeatedly suggested counseling because she thought he needed to talk to someone, but he dismissed the conversation every time. He felt like seeing a therapist would make him look crazy. Still, she knew deeply that he needed the help. She thought no one else would be able to get through to him like professional counseling could since they were trained to manage behavior like his.

Wendell's actions didn't bother Monet as much until he directed them at her. He often said things that were out of line and disrupted their relationship. He would say things like, "*You're lucky you even have someone like me,*" or "*You're not even all that.*" Whenever he got mad, he would call her bad names. If she unintentionally hurt him, he would plot to get back at her and hurt her worse. Before he met Monet, his aggressive tones, sarcastic remarks, and disrespectful words were the reasons he scared away other girls. This was the very thing she was warned about when she first met him. He wasn't a physical abuser to women like his father was. He vowed never to hurt a woman how his mom was hurt, but his anger about his parents' situation led him to be an emotional and verbal abuser. This type of abuse was just as bad as physical abuse.

One afternoon, Monet called Wendell and convinced him to go on a date for a walk at a nearby park. When they met up, she gave him a very embracing hug as if she had been feeling down and needed the hug to make her feel better and relieve some of her pain. He smiled with unsureness of what could be wrong. He knew she wasn't acting like herself lately, but he couldn't figure out why. Monet was stressing about if she wanted to continue dating him or move on with her life. She figured counseling would be worth a try if he would agree to attend with her.

As she gazed at the beautiful flowers, bright green grass, and a few kids running around, she took a deep breath. She inhaled the fresh air as her mind drifted into deep thought. She remembered a speech she listened in the past. *"Keep running the race. Don't give up! Don't become small-minded. Change your circle and push toward success."*

Wendell observed her for a moment before asking, "Baby, what is wrong?"

At that moment, she felt his question was perfect timing for her to express her thoughts. It was time for him to either help push them toward a better relationship or leave her life. Monet turned towards him and gave him another hug. She kissed his lips softly three times. When she opened her eyes, she realized his eyes were closed as if he was passionately enjoying her kisses and embracing the moment they were sharing. Her strategy was to get him as calm as possible.

When she knew she had gotten him to a peaceful place, she said, "I have been going through a lot. I think it would be helpful if you would join me in therapy."

He quickly said, "I told you no before. I am not going to no therapy sessions."

Monet couldn't hold back anymore. She began to explain the things he had done that caused her pain. She mentioned everything from his insecurities that he covers

up with protection to his anger which has only brought
Monet misery. The relationship didn't feel so beautiful
anymore. His attitude was like a storm in the midst of her
trying to breathe fresh air.

He said, "You take your mental butt there yourself.
You need it anyway."

The words echoed in her ear and brought tears to
her eyes. The nice guy she knew had become a monster.
Monet knew he had issues within himself and that he was
always making excuses for his actions. Her friends would
tell her she deserves better. Still, her heart wouldn't allow
her to let go. Monet felt she could help change him since
she knew the pain he had endured in his childhood. She
thought if she walked away, she was giving up on someone
who needed her. The kinder side of him helped her hold on
to their relationship for as long as she did.

On a good day, Wendell's personality could melt
anyone's heart. He was an affectionate lover. At times, he
could make her feel as if she had no flaws. He could make
her believe that she was beautiful no matter what
predicament she faced. On the other hand, once he became
upset, his temper allowed strong aggression to take over.
He didn't want to be that way. But, in his mind, all he knew
was to fight to protect who he is and what he has left in life.
Monet didn't like him as a boyfriend anymore, but she
loved him as a friend. She learned something from him that
no words, advice, or speech could teach her. As she walked
away with tears in her eyes, he followed. She explained that
he was not the one for her. If he could make the situation
easier for them both by leaving her alone, she would be
grateful.

"What did you just say to me?" he asked.

A part of her feared what he was thinking. The other part hesitated because deep down, leaving him was hard to do.

She mumbled, "It hurts me to walk away, Wendell, but staying hurts worse."

He laughed and told her, "You are crazy if you think you would be happy without me."

In her mind, she knew he was saying that to make her mad. Still, her heart was aching. As Wendell's insults and threats began to fade, her mind began to think back on a previous encounter she had with a young lady she met at a party. The young lady's personality was just like Wendell's. Monet thought back to how she tried to get Wendell some help the first month she knew he had gotten hurt by his father. She had researched the situation and knew the signs. So, when she met the young lady, it was easy to see through her smile.

During their encounter, she told Monet, "My dude chokes me and smacks me around a little bit. He puts me in my place all the time. If he came in here and said shut up, I'm going to sit back and shut up! Sometimes it throws me off, but a lot of times, it turns me on."

Monet paused as she tried to gather herself and think about what to say next without offending the young lady. She also wanted to give her a bit of wisdom. Monet didn't speak quickly enough, and the lady got lost within the crowd as everyone was off to do their own thing. As the evening came close to an end, she saw the young lady gathering her things to leave. Monet stopped her.

"Excuse me. Now, call me crazy, but what you said to me doesn't sit right with me. I feel I should say something."

The girl looked confused and said, "What?"

Monet said, "I can't let you leave and not talk to you. I'm not in a place to judge, and that is not what I am attempting to do. I'm here at this beautiful empowerment event, and it's only right for sisters to help one another out. May you and I talk please?"

The girl had a confused look on her face not sure where Monet was going with this. Monet could feel the negativity from the young lady and explained her position.

"I'm in a group that counsels women and young girls who have been abused or damaged, and I feel that people need to hear your voice."

As her face started to smooth over, Monet asked about her background. The young lady didn't care to elaborate. However, Monet's tone was respectful and sisterly. The young lady could either respectfully respond or respectfully decline. She realized that Monet meant her no harm, so she agreed to talk. Monet began by asking her name.

"Please call me Mini," she said.

Monet wasn't sure why she gave her nickname or a fake name at an empowerment event that could change her life, but she respectfully called her the name provided. As Mini told her things she witnessed growing up as a child, things that were out of her control, her story was a lot like Wendell's story. It all made sense as to why she thought being mistreated was okay. Mini was a name her boyfriend gave her and told her to use. It sounded almost as if he was pimping her. Monet explained to her the difference in accepting dominant men who will stand firm and protect her and not someone who will physically bring her harm. She needed someone to provide for her and make sure she was covered with their best interest at heart for her. She also clarified how she should never confuse this type of man with a man whose intentions were to pimp her and use the money to control her. Instead, she needed someone to profess his love to her as his queen and not mislead her to believe that because he said he loves her, it gave him the right to think he could mistreat her in public or in private.

As Monet walked away with so many thoughts in her mind, she couldn't believe she had ended her relationship with Wendell. However, she knew she had done all she could. She wondered if he would get it right or if he would harm himself, or someone else. Her mind was clouded. Nevertheless, she came to her senses and knew that the only one who could help him recover from his past was God. Monet's heart never allowed her to see the bad in people.

Reminder:

As parents, practicing the behaviors you want your children to learn is an important job that requires a disciplined mindset that is focused on applying the principles, you intend for them to follow. Seeing the different love languages enacted affects how a child's love develops. A child's first role model is their parents. They grow up under their leadership and guidance while learning and soaking up all that they give through words and actions. Children watch what people laugh at just the same as they watch the things that mentally, physically, and spiritually break a person down. They see the fighting and yelling and even the cupcake lovely nights. They notice when mommy and daddy get excited and dressed up for date night. They also notice when there is an awkward silence in the room, when moods change, and the simple things that no one thinks a child notices.

Children are so much smarter than most adults can imagine. Their minds are like sponges soaking up everything around them. Even when the challenging moments are supposed to be kept hidden, sometimes children pick up on those actions, too. It's confusing to a child when parents do and say things in front of children and then disciplines them for repeating those actions. When your actions are hypocritical to your instructions for them, it gives the children the impression that it's okay to do those things. Furthermore, it leaves them with no standards of behavior.

Children are very observant. Therefore, not much can get past them unless they are asleep, not home, or otherwise pre-occupied. For example, as Monet tried to sleep, the sounds in the hallway made her curious. That is the case in many situations. You must be aware that kids are paying attention even in moments like a car ride. They might be playing on their iPad, listening to music, or simply looking out the window as you are taking a call while driving, or talking with someone in the passenger seat. However, they hear your conversation, and their minds wonder what you could be discussing.

Children also watch how to accept love and how to handle heartbreak. If a child sees his or her daddy strike their mom just as Wendell did, it doesn't mean that they will repeat those actions. It doesn't even mean they will accept those actions from anyone. However, seeing such action conflicts with acceptable words spoken and causes confusion for the child. Sons grow up hating the bad things their father did to their mom, and they develop an anger issue that transfers to his relationship when he meets a woman. If she pushes him to the edge of anger, he may find himself striking the woman and realizing he has now become his father. This is not always the case, but it is something that many children face.

After witnessing the abuse of your parent, I can understand how such anger can trigger the sadness you remembered from those times but understand that the pain your mother endured is the same pain that you would be inflicting on someone if you repeat those actions. Don't cause that pain to another woman. So many daughters grow up and enter toxic relationships without understanding why she can't stray from bad boys or false love. Truthfully, she sometimes attracts those people because her heart is attracted to what she knows and what she has seen. Even though the false love and bad relationships were all she saw, as bad as she may have hated it, it's the lifestyle that she learned and understands. Unfortunately, generational curses and bad habits can sometimes be challenging to break.

Let's not just single out the ones that went through traumatic situations when they were younger. Some children became the total opposite of their parents as they got older because they didn't want to be a product of their environment. Some girls were raised well like Monet, yet she witnessed that heartbreak and abuse outside the home. She became drawn into that life wanting to see why people are attracted to that lifestyle. They try to find a man's good side and attempt to make it better. Change only comes when those individuals desire the change and decide to change on their own time and terms.

To the youth, please tell yourself it's time to break the generational curse. Change your mindset to know that your life is yours to control and does not have to be the product of where you grow up, how you grew up, or what you experienced growing up. Most times, parents are not aware of the impact they have on the life of the child. Still, the cycle does not have to continue. You may not have received an apology from your parents. Here's the apology on their behalf to help you release that pain you are harboring. I am sorry! I am sorry that you witnessed bad decisions, unacceptable actions, and bad lessons that should have been good. The pain from your past can heal, but it starts with you first releasing yourself from all things you had no control over. You must allow yourself to be free of generational curses so that you can reach your greatest potential. You cannot allow your pain to affect your future, so please seek further assistance to get past that cycle of past pain.

If you are a parent, it is not too late to restructure yourself, your home, and your love life. Don't be afraid or too prideful to apologize to the children you have hurt. Children need to be aware that they were not at fault in the actions seen around them. That pain is embedded in their hearts leading them to search for the wrong love or become the wrong lover. Let's start the change that can impact future generations today!

Question:

Have you ever read The Five Love Languages *by Gary Chapman? If not, read the book or look up the free online quiz to assess your love language. Keep your love language in mind when dating, and consider the love language of your significant other. If you have experienced negative love, write a prayer that God brings about change that will impact your life positively. If it's positive, thank God and ask Him to help you to stay focused.*

Chapter 2

Are You Self-loving or Self-sabotaging?

1 Peter 3:3-4

"Your beauty should not come from outward adornment, such as elaborate hairstyles, wearing of gold jewelry, or fine clothes. Rather, it should be that of your inner self, the unfading beauty of a gentle and quiet spirit, which is of great worth in God's sight."

As the sun kissed Noel's face through the slightly cracked open window in her bedroom, she turned from her stomach to her back and stretched widely. She reached over to her nightstand to check the time on her clock. It was 7:21 a.m., but her alarm had not gone off. She panicked when she realized she hadn't set her alarm.

"I'm usually out the door by now. Dang! I'm going to miss my ride," Noel said jumping up from her bed and quickly making her way to her closet to get ready for work.

Luckily for her, she prepares her outfits for work the night before. She grabbed her phone and went straight to Pandora to play some music to help speed along her daily routine. The music gives her an extra energy boost. Although she was late, she didn't want to move outside of her normal routine. She didn't want to forget something important.

"Of all days, today is not the day to be late," she said.

This week her internship was coming to an end, and she was praying to get hired for a permanent position. She wanted every action to be on point. As she was putting on her pants, with one leg in and struggling to get the other leg in, a text came in on her phone. She hurriedly pulled her pants up without fastening them and ran towards her phone to make sure it wasn't her ride. The text was long and didn't come from her ride. She didn't bother with reading it at that moment. She knew if she did, she would be delaying her time more. The text came from an ex-boyfriend. She decided she would wait to read and respond - if she even responded at all. Noel threw her phone on the bed and ran to the bathroom. She grabbed her toothbrush and turned on the water to brush her teeth. Once the water was steaming hot, she started washing her face. She could hear her mother yelling but couldn't make out what she was saying.

Her mother yelled, "Noel your ride is here!" but the running water drowned out the sound of her voice. Since Noel was rushing, she didn't bother yelling back. She fastened her pants, put on her shirt, and started to put on her shoes when she heard her mom yelling again.

"Noel?"

With aggravation from trying to rush, she yelled back, "Yes?"

Her mom didn't catch on to the attitude. Instead, she asked, "Did you hear me? Your ride is here!"

Noel responded, "Okay. I'm coming."

She grabbed her stuff and ran outside to the car. She was full of apologies and explaining the wait. Ms. Marie was very understanding. She didn't mind.

"It's okay, Love. You are usually waiting on my late behind. I'm finally on time for a change."

Usually, Noel was outside waiting for Ms. Marie, so she knew that it was simply a mistake. They both laughed as Noel got in the car. She fastened her seatbelt, and Ms. Marie pulled off. Simultaneously, they pulled their sun visors down to block the sun from beaming in their faces. Noel glanced into the mirror of the sun visor and noticed that a rash was forming under her eye. The rash was big enough for anyone looking at her to notice. She had seen it when she was in the bathroom, but it didn't look as bad as it did at that moment. She hadn't paid as much attention last night or earlier this morning due to her fast-paced life. She only noticed the rash because she was still. The sight of the rash quickly changed her mood. Noel had sensitive skin, so a gentle touch would cause her skin to break out. It was something about that mirror she couldn't stand, so she put the sun visor up and closed her eyes for a moment to fight back the tears.

She asked Ms. Marie, "Do you have any unscented lotion or Vaseline."

"Let me check."

As she looked in the armrest and the glove compartment, there was no lotion or anything for skin. Noel thought that maybe her skin was dry and looked worse because it was dry. The way her face looked made her confidence low. She couldn't even dodge the sun thinking that the exposure could make it worse. Tears flowed down her face from the sadness she felt. As the soft beat from the music of Ms. Marie's playlist became familiar, the tears started flowing nonstop from Noel's eye. Ms. Marie was looking forward and paying attention to the road as she nodded her head to the song. So, she didn't notice Noel was crying.

As they got closer to their workplace, they both realized that traffic was lighter than usual. They were thirty minutes early, so they decided to stop for breakfast. Maria asked Noel what she wanted to eat. Noel loved the idea of having breakfast and not settling for muffins and coffee. However, she wasn't in the best mood today. Marie looked overseeing that her eyes were pink with a glossy look. She turned the music all the way down and asked Noel, "What is going on?"

Noel didn't respond.

"Is everything okay?" she asked again, but Noel was still quiet.

"I'm hoping your eyes are pink from allergies and not tears, Noel," Ms. Marie said.

Marie is a friend of the family. She helped Noel get a job with her as an intern fresh out of high school. She always talked to Marie because she felt close to her and Noel was very comfortable with talking to Marie about anything. However, but at that moment, she felt her tears were too dramatic.

She asked again "What's the matter?"

Noel sighed and said, "My face… This rash has made me feel ugly."

Ms. Maria looked over at her with a frown on her face and said, "Are you kidding me? You are so beautiful inside and out."

Noel didn't bother to believe her words because she felt it was her job to say nice things to her since she was a friend of the family. She saw the rash herself, and she thought there was nothing pretty about that. The rashes that magically appear on her face had become the comedy show to some, the movie for others, and had caused others to stare. Noel was sad and. Even though Ms. Marie told her how pretty she was, she didn't feel the beauty. She could only see the rash that caused her to cringe at the sight of it.

"We can stop at the store and get you some ointment," Ms. Marie said as she put the car in reverse to leave the parking lot. "I wasn't acting like I didn't see the rash. I really didn't, Noel."

She drove to the CVS down the street from their job. Noel wiped her face, and they got out of the car. As she closed her door, she saw herself again in the glass window. Every time she saw the rash, it seemed to be getting worse. It wasn't as bad as she was thinking. However, Marie understood how it could make her self-esteem shift. As they walked past people in the store, Ms. Marie noticed Noel constantly putting her hands in her face to block people from seeing it.

She said to Noel softly, "Baby, it's not as bad as you think. Besides, we don't know these people. You are making it worse with your hands on it just to shield from these strangers."

Noel moved her hands, but her heart dropped. In her mind, everyone was staring at her. They purchased the ointment and got in the car to head to work. She didn't even get out of the parking lot fully before she cleaned the area of her face and applied the ointment.

She knew she had to get it together for work, but the rash had her feeling insecure. They walked into the building, and the front desk specialist greeted them and gave them their list of tasks for the day. As they looked over the list, they realized it wasn't as many items listed as it normally would be. Ms. Maria knew they would have time to talk. She wanted to give Noel some encouragement and advice. At Noel's age, her generation was partying, smoking, hanging out, and chilling at every function. Ms. Maria didn't want her to give up on her future if the internship ended. She also didn't want her to allow her peers to change her mindset and make her believe she must do those things to have fun.

As they walked down the hall in silence to the break room to get their breakfast, Noel didn't have a taste for anything. As Ms. Marie fixed her coffee with three French vanilla creamers, she grabbed Noel a banana so that she could put something on her stomach. She knew that when Noel was frustrated or overworking herself, she tended not to eat. Noel was looking out into the hall and noticed a guy named Kevin walking into the building. As they made eye contact, she quickly looked away and raised her hand to cover her face. Noel had a huge crush on Kevin ever since she first started the internship. She would see him and become fixated the moment he came around. She was crushing on him big time. Although she wished to have the courage and confidence to approach him, she went through a major stage of battling insecurities.

Noel knew Kevin was the ladies' man. As good looking as he is, it didn't surprise her. Noel has seen some of the women in the office boldly flirting with him. She felt she could never have a chance with him. She didn't believe she was his type. The girls he looked at lustfully were women who looked like models. They had a body that was curvy in all the right places and skin that was flawlessly clear. They looked as if they were without flaws. People admired Noel as an individual. They loved her heart and personality. They admired the way she followed her dreams. When she would look over her desk and see Kevin smiling a little harder than normal at some of their coworkers, it would make her so upset. She would wonder why her face had to be breaking out.

For so many years, even amongst family, she felt like the ugly duckling and the outcast. When Noel was younger, people judged her about her physical appearance, fashion, and not being cool enough to hang. Her mind was too advanced for the crowd she wished to join. She didn't get called on or asked out on dates. No matter the reason, it didn't feel good to accept being ignored. She couldn't understand why her. When she would explain the situation to people, they would tell her she's different. But, she didn't want to be different. She wanted to be accepted. She thought if her loved ones didn't accept her, why would the world. She always looked at her flaws and wondered if that's why guys didn't choose her. She didn't quite understand what made people count her out. That lack of understanding allowed the insecurities within her to grow.

Ms. Marie was sitting at the table in the break room drinking her coffee. She noticed Noel looking at the handsome man, Mr. Kevin. The company was against coworkers being in a romantically involved in a relationship. Ms. Marie thought that since the internship was coming to an end, Noel could see if he wanted to pursue more. *"Noel's day would turn around,"* Ms. Marie thought. She second-guessed herself deciding for Noel without discussing with her first. She felt Noel might take it as if Marie persuaded him, and that would only hurt her more. She didn't know how Noel would feel, but she thought it was worth the try.

They finally left the break room and decided they would start their workday. As Noel was sitting at her desk, she remembered the long text that she received earlier that day. She decided to read it. It came from the number she saved as "NO LIAR ZONE." She didn't want to read the message, but she saw something big in it - an apology. She didn't want the apology to take him back, but she did want him to realize he messed up. A few months ago, her ex-boyfriend degraded her as a young woman. She went to visit her friend Mya, and they walked to the park. Her ex-boyfriend happened to be at the same park. It wasn't a coincidence because they lived in the same neighborhood.

As they walked inside the recreational building, Noel noticed her ex-boyfriend was acting a little strange. He asked her friend to hold his phone while he played basketball with his friends. It didn't make sense that he asked her while Noel was standing right there.

Mya said, "Uh oh. Someone just texted his phone."

Noel was a little terrified to go through his stuff. She knew he was crazy, and she didn't know how far he would go.

Noel replied, "Oh, well. Leave it alone."

Mya said, "No, girl! It's a picture. I'm opening it!"

Noel's ex-boyfriend was not the brightest; he never put a passcode on his device. The picture was of a girl standing in the mirror naked and looking stank. Noel's heart started pounding as they backed out of the message. She realized there were multiple females he had been conversing with and sending nudes. Noel's relationship with him was too innocent compared to the other girls she saw in his phone.

She asked her friend, "Please delete my pictures and texts." Mya obliged. Then, Noel said, "Oh yeah. Delete the call log and my number. Hopefully, he doesn't remember it by heart."

Mya deleted everything Noel asked her to and put the phone down.

"Dang, he wild for that. Are you okay?" Mya asked.

Noel wanted to cry, but she knew something wasn't right about him and how he acted. She responded carelessly, "Yeah. I'm thankful to know."

As the game ended, he asked Mya for his phone. She handed it over to him. He had other messages come through during that time, so he couldn't tell that they had been looking through his phone. He asked Noel if he could talk to her in private.

She said, "Why can't you talk in front of Mya?"

He knew something wasn't right because she was usually so in love and fell for anything, but her mouth was smart and filled with attitude.

He said, "Because I don't want to."

They got up and went into a private room.

He asked her, "Why do you have on those tiny shorts showing off your butt?"

In her mind, she wanted to say, *"You're concerned about my wardrobe but talking to multiple women."* She didn't owe him any explanation, so she didn't say anything at all.

He grabbed her arm forcefully and said, "Go in the house and quit acting like a little slut. You look just like your friends, but you 're not giving me any. I know all of you are hot in the pants. So, you must be having sex with someone."

Noel scolded, "Get off me, and don't you ever feel like it's okay to touch me like that again! That's a warning."

As he grabbed her and tried to pick her up, she pushed all her weight to the ground so that he couldn't. He started to drag her to the girl's restroom. As she fought against him, tears began to fall. He continued to drag her. As she got to the doorway, she held the wall. He hit her hands and told her to stop looking dumb and being dramatic.

Noel yelled, "Get off me!"

As he got her in the bathroom, he inserted a finger into her treasure box and told her, "Stop acting like you don't love me."

He began to force three fingers inside of her, causing her pain.

With tears in her eyes, Noel said, "Get off me now. This doesn't feel good to me. It hurts."

"Be quiet," he said.

As he was getting ready to take her pants off, she yelled, "If you do this to me, this will not be a secret. I will consider this rape."

The word rape echoed in his ear. He dropped Noel and told her that she was a childish heifer. Noel didn't care. She was just happy he didn't continue further. Moments later, after Mya saw him alone, she came into the bathroom and saw Noel crying. She didn't even ask questions. She went back out the door. Noel finally got herself together and went back outside only to realize Mya and her ex-boyfriend were neck and neck arguing. The family came out, and the small argument turned into a fight. During that time, Noel felt bad to have her family reacting like that. She felt it was all her fault. When the fight ended, the ex-boyfriend yelled that he had been dealing with another girl and Noel was his toy. His words hurt her to the core, but she was happy to escape and not become a victim of rape. That incident was why she was hesitant to read his message. Why was he messaging her? The message read:

"Noel, I am sure I'm the last person you want to hear from at all. I messed up, and I don't know if you need

to hear this to move on. You weren't the problem at all. It was me. My mind was messed up and in the wrong place. The drugs took over me, and I ruined a lot in my life because of it. Not that you care, but I have a little girl on the way who will love me during my dirt, and some man will love her in the future. I don't want her to fall for a boy like myself.

"I want to say I'm so sorry for what I've done. This message is not to get back with you. I just wanted to say you are a great girl. You are so close to perfect that it's crazy. The right man will be blessed to have you. I messed up, but I hope you don't allow that to keep you from letting the right one love you. I can't say this enough, but I'm sorry. Take care."

Noel was stuck. She didn't know how to feel. She needed that closure because of the pain that made her fault herself in the past. She often thought, *"Maybe he cheated because I wasn't having sex. Maybe I wasn't spoiling him enough."* Many more thoughts crossed her mind. She blamed him because he was wrong, but she questioned herself as well. She listened to the sad story in the beginning and tried to love on him different from the way his ex-girlfriend loved him. However, he didn't appreciate Noel. That left her feeling how she felt as a child - not good enough. She fixed her emotions, exited out the message, and got back to work.

Noel noticed Marie in Kevin's office, but she couldn't tell what was being said. She thought it could've been about work, but she noticed they both looked her way. She didn't know if it was because they noticed her looking at them, but she instantly looked away with slight embarrassment. As she pondered how noticeable she must have been, she wondered how crazy she looked when she kept looking away so fast knowing their eyes had met.

Ms. Marie grabbed a folder and headed back to her desk. About twenty minutes later, Noel noticed Kevin standing nice and tall as he gathered himself. He looked a bit nervous. His skin was silky smooth, and he looked freshly dipped in milk chocolate with a smile that was perfectly straight with his pearly white teeth. Kevin had a fresh haircut. He had on a suit and tie and looked like he was straight out of a fashion magazine.

As he started walking towards Noel, her heart dropped to her feet, and she instantly started to get hot. She reached over to turn off the heat thinking that would help, but no luck. There was a soft knock at her door as if he barely touched the door.

"Come in!" Noel said.

As he entered her office, she gazed at his physical appearance and fell deeper into lust as she became intoxicated by his beautiful scent that she loved. He had on a cologne that smelled like white amber. While she was in deep thought, he asked her about an assignment she was given. She had perfected everything she learned, but she couldn't get to her file fast enough because of her nerves. Truthfully, Kevin wasn't there for the assignment. Ms. Marie had told Kevin that Noel was interested in him. She informed him that Noel was delicate. Kevin didn't mind getting to know her for himself. So, he decided to use work to spark a conversation with her. Noel didn't know why he needed her to review the files with him. They all had access to the same system. However, she didn't care about the reason. If he was speaking to her, she was flattered. As she navigated the computer, Kevin's phone rang. Someone needed him, which was a relief for Noel. He placed the paper he was holding down on her desk and left his number with a note that said: Lunch date today.

As her heart pounded with anxiety, her smile lit up. She tried her hardest to act normal. She was so excited for this date but nervous like she was interviewing for her job all over again. Lunch was in an hour, and she knew she wouldn't be able to focus on work. So, she took a break to go to the restroom and freshen up. She texted the number he gave her and said, "I'll be there for lunch." She was so excited but looking at her face again made her wonder if he even saw the rash. She wondered if he would be focused on her facial imperfections while they were at lunch. Although she was upset about her face, she knew this was her moment. Therefore, she wouldn't dismiss the date.

As the last few minutes slowly passed, Noel straightened her desk for the fifth time. She made her last call on the list for the day and made sure that she would have an easy day after lunch. When it was time to go on her lunch date, Kevin left out before her. A few seconds later, he texted her and said, "I'm in the black Porsche on the side. Don't want people being nosy."

Noel notified Ms. Marie that she would return in an hour. As she was walking to the car, her heart was racing. She looked at her phone the whole walk to the car so she wouldn't feel that she was looking crazy. When she got in the car, she loved his ride. It had all black leather interior with a hint of red. He had a little hood to the businessman she was used to seeing every day. He was bumping rap music. Although the car was nice, Noel wasn't the type of girl that was impressed with the material things. She liked him for him. Her anxiety had her shaking so bad that Kevin even noticed and asked was she okay. It was seventy-eight degrees outside, but the quickest response she could give was, "Yes. I'm just cold."

He jokingly said, "What? Are you anemic?"

The great thing was that she could say yes and not be telling another lie. As Kevin looked at her, Noel wanted to look back into his eyes, but she was too shy. She looked down at her hands and began playing with her nails.

He asked, "Are you always this shy?"

She smiled and said, "Yeah until I get to know you more, I guess."

He noticed she had dimples and complimented them. It was like fireworks in her heart and stomach to receive the compliment. She tried not to come off desperate, so she kept it brief and simply thanked him. She didn't want to pour out her heart in words scaring him away, but she didn't know if saying very little gave off the impression she wasn't interested. This dating thing was new to Noel.

He said, "Noel, stop being shy. You are so beautiful."

As much as she wanted to receive the compliment, she became sad instead.

He could tell and asked, "What just changed your emotion?"

She explained that another guy she had dealt with degraded her character when he was upset. He only complimented her so he could make her feel good after he hurt her. All the compliments he gave her were fake.

Kevin replied, "I am not him. Give me a hug."

She reached over and gave him a church hug. He took matters into his own hands and hugged her tightly as if he knew her, missed her, or had been dating her for a while.

Noel didn't mind it though. His scent and his strong manly structure caressing her body made her feel safe and even loved for the moment. As he looked her in the eyes, she looked away quickly feeling embarrassed. She remembered the rash that was forming. *"He's going to laugh at me. I know he thinks I'm ugly now,"* she thought to herself.

Noel didn't want to be disappointed, but she couldn't continue to assume, so she asked, "Why did you give me that look?"

He smiled. "Your eyes are so beautiful."

She couldn't help but be happy with his response. Before he could make a joke or say anything to hurt her, she mentioned the scar developing on her face.

"I thought you were looking at this stupid rash under my eye."

He said, "I saw that, but it didn't bother me. I was looking at your eyes."

She smiled back and noticed he was coming towards her. He kissed her, and her eyes closed. As he kissed her more, he felt the opportunity to feel on her breasts. She wanted to say, "No, I'm not ready for that yet," but her flesh was loving how he made her feel. She never felt accepted, and for the first time, it was flowing so naturally. Noel couldn't control her emotions anymore. She had been crying all morning, and here she was on a date with her crush. As he continued to kiss her and caress her, his hands eased inside her pants. The fear of what her ex-boyfriend did crept back into her mind. She grabbed his hand to stop him and informed him that she was a virgin and sex was too soon.

He said, "We won't have sex. I want you to feel good."

As she noticed his finger twinging in her treasure box, the moisture increased. She had never experienced her body responding in that way. It caught her off guard, but she loved it all at the same time. It was nothing like the time her ex-boyfriend touched her. She wondered was he using her because he knew how much she liked him, or if he was genuinely feeling the chemistry. She knew that she had to stop him before he assumed she was an easy target. She grabbed his hands to make him stop. He respectfully did as she asked which made her extremely happy. He couldn't leave without telling her how good and moist her treasure box felt. Although she smiled, she knew that sexual activity before marriage was against her religion, so she felt bad. Kevin's phone rang, as much as he didn't want to stop, he had no choice. It was the manager. Their hearts raced thinking someone had seen them together. He turned the music down and asked her to be quiet. Then, he answered the phone.

The office manager said, "I know you are on lunch break. I do apologize for calling during this time. I just wanted to inform you that the regional manager would be in after lunch. So, be prepared before you even come back."

The office manager always preps the team to be on their best behavior and show off their skills. Although it was for his work team only, not the interns, Noel was happy to know he would be there so that she could prepare, too! The regional manager usually observes everything. They decided to cut their break short. Kevin pulled into Wendy's lot and parked for a moment to talk to Noel. She was so happy the scar was on the right side close to the window; he couldn't see it well. He admitted that he saw it but didn't care. But she was still ashamed and didn't like the way it looked.

Kevin knew it was something about her that was different. However, if she had said it, he would have run away from her. He didn't like when girls announced that they were different. He felt they were either lying or thought they were better. Noel's heart is so big that it even showed during her silence. The qualities that she battled with accepting were things he liked more. They could barely eat because the conversations were so intriguing. They smiled and had a good time. He kept apologizing for having to shift plans. Even though the date was quick and inexpensive, the quality time with her crush meant everything to her. She couldn't wait to get back to the office to share her happiness with Ms. Marie.

When they got back to the office, he allowed her to walk in first. He stayed in his car and checked a few of his emails to see what the topic would be in the office to stall on time. Their policy was no dating other staff members mainly because they didn't want distractions in the office. Furthermore, if things don't work out, they didn't want conflict in the workplace. About twelve minutes after Noel entered the office, he came in behind her with different bags from what she had. As happy as she was, she couldn't show it. She wanted to talk about it with Ms. Marie, but the regional manager was in the conference room not too far from them. So, Noel chose to stay low key at her desk. She looked to see what work she could complete since she finished up her workload before lunch. As she was working and listening to music, the glow on her face showed that her lunch date made her day. This was a huge deal, and she couldn't stay quiet any longer.

She picked up her desk phone, dialed Ms. Marie, and told her, "I am so pleased with my date. He's a charmer inside and out."

Ms. Marie smiled with joy that Noel's date was good. Noel knew that going into details would disturb the conversation, so she kept it innocent. Ms. Marie wasn't happy that she put her emotions in the hands of a man. She was simply happy that tears were not filling Noel's eyes anymore.

Reminder:

Self-love is key! People count you out for many reasons. You must first love yourself so much that you become unbothered to jealousy and envy. Everybody won't like you or respect your name. No one is perfect. However, insecurities allow you to lose focus because you compare yourself to others. It may challenge you at times, but you must know that beauty first starts within. Asking for someone else's season of life can cause pressure for you within your own. You might sometimes look back at your situations wonder why you went through certain situations, but it's because you asked for those things.

Keep in mind that people don't always show the storms they face. Everyone has flaws, including the people you admire. They went through a point in their lives when they wished their butt was bigger, stomach flat, nose smaller, hair curly, or even that their skin was smoother. You must learn to accept who you are, own it, and love every detail of yourself. Your true identity makes you unique. When you embrace yourself and build your confidence, people will respect you much more. You will then see that you don't need someone to build your self-esteem. The right person usually overlooks the things that worry you. Please stand in the mirror and stare at the beauty God gave to you as a blessing. Tell yourself, "I AM BEAUTIFUL!" You truly are! Continue to say it until you feel it and believe it! You are beautiful, fearfully, and wonderfully made as a gift from God.

Question:

What flaw do you trouble with and why? Write it down and then add: "Despite my flaws, I AM BEAUTIFUL." Say it and believe it!

_____

_____

_____

_____

_____

_____

_____

_____

_____

_____

_____

_____

_____

_____

_____

_____

_____

_____

_____

Chapter 3

What Do You Value Most in a Relationship?

Proverbs 13:20

"Walk with the wise and become wise, for a companion of fools suffer from harm."

Leon, DeAngelo, Jerome, Darryl, and James were handsome, strong black men that had a voice of power. They had a background of protection and zero tolerance for disrespect from anyone. They were courageous with strong, undefeated attitudes, all of which surrounded Shannon. They often treated her as a baby, but she was far from one. She was just considered the baby of the bunch which to them, is delicate. When the guys were growing up, their second job has always been to protect Shannon. She knew that if anyone ever crossed her path negatively, she had a mob behind her that wasn't taking any mess.

Family gatherings were changing over the years. The fun times started becoming depressing. The family was becoming more focused on themselves. They were either not making time for each other or keeping the feuds growing. They did not realize how their attitudes towards different situations were rubbing against everyone's spirit. The smiles became so fake that the youth began to look towards their friends and their families as family. They just wished the drama would stop against each other.

On Easter Sunday, the family decided to come together at Aunt Leslie's house. Surprisingly, everyone was excited about this gathering. The family usually divides themselves at every event. The children were usually nosy, and the adults would have to tell them to go to the other room and stay in a child's place. This time Shannon's mother came prepared with games and activities for the youth. The kids were confined to one part of the house. The teens were off to the side in their cell phones. Some were playing games and cards down in the basement. The men were somewhere talking about "men things" like sports, women, and vehicles. Of course, the women were not too far from the kitchen with all their latest stories, reality shows, relationships, fashion, and more. Then, there were the elderly which Shannon refers to as the Jewels of the bunch. They were sitting in their lovely corner getting pampered.

Shannon was in the late teenage years becoming a young adult so that she would be everywhere in the house. As she was upstairs making a personal call, her sister came into the room and told her that she was needed downstairs. Shannon and her sister weren't as close as she wished. So, their conversation was usually short. Part of the reason was Shannon's fault. She was going through puberty and trying to find herself. The moment she tried to be sneaky with a boy in her early years, her younger sister told on her. Shannon shut down from that moment forward. She didn't think she could trust her sister with her darkest secrets.

Although they had grown up since then, Shannon still believed her sister wouldn't understand the things she was going through in her life. So, she never shared. As Shannon made her way down two flights of stairs, she looked everywhere to see who called for her. No one seemed to have needed her anymore. As she got ready to go back upstairs, the aromas filled her nose from the kitchen. She couldn't help but see how the food was coming along.

They were doing an amazing job. They had food on the grill, and they were cooking inside as well. It was almost looking like the Thanksgiving menu. They were putting their foot in that food.

There were certain signature dishes that the Jewels must make and could never be duplicated no matter who tried. Their food has and will forever be loved by everyone who tries it. Shannon's cousin stopped the attention of the food for a moment asking if she could have something to drink. During that time, Shannon was ready to taste anything she could. They couldn't help but to give her a piece of chicken and told her to move.

"Don't treat me like that," she said jokingly.

They told Shannon she needed to go back upstairs because she was eating up everything and saving none for anyone else to eat. Shannon laughed at the comment as her aunt took the floor and started singing to the soft tone that was playing from the radio. She turned up the volume, and the ladies of the house tuned in as well. There was an echo that filled the home from the sound of a doorbell. Surprisingly none even cared or bothered to let anyone know. The kids remained focused on their activities. Shannon's little cousin, Jayla, was making her way down the stairs from the restroom when she noticed a young man at the door. She ran to the kitchen in full of excitement.

"The door! The door! Someone is at the door!"

Shannon was so distracted by all that was going on around her that she forgot that her phone was left upstairs on the charger. As she walked out of the kitchen and around the corner, her great aunt, Leslie, who owns the house was already greeting the guest. As Leslie took his jacket, Shannon was standing a few feet back with cheeks the color of roses. It was her boo that she claims to be her friend. Shannon gets shy when he's around but loves his presence.

She said, "Hey Mike!"

"Hey. I tried calling twice but no answer," Mike said.

As she checked her pockets walking towards him, she replied, "Aw man. I left my phone upstairs after I hung up. The family called me down."

He said with a smile, "It's cool!"

As they finished that conversation and hugged, Shannon got butterflies. Mike was the first boy she ever thought to bring to meet her family. She didn't know what to expect. As she led him around the corner to start the introductions, her heart was pounding.

She looked back at him and asked, "Are you okay."

He smiled and said, "Yeah," as if he had no nervous bones.

She first introduced him to the children because their bubbly spirits would give her some laughter and peace. The kids spoke to him as if they already knew him. Jayla was one of the youngest of all the cousins. She doesn't do well with accepting any new faces. She would either give her shy personality or go the extreme of crying if someone got too close to her. She's been like that since she was a baby. Mike reached his hand out seeing if she would give him a high five. Without hesitation, Jayla hit his hand extremely hard, excited to play with him. That moment alone made Shannon's heart melt because that was new for Jayla.

The other children started speaking, full of excitement to show him their Easter projects. Once one showed theirs, the others couldn't help but show theirs. Shannon thought it was a good icebreaker.

She made her way to the teenagers who were stuck in their phones.

She broke the ice and said, "Y'all, this is my friend Mike."

The group shared a joke saying, "What? Somebody wants you?"

They all laughed and then started asking what he did when they realized he was so buff. He told them he was a football player, and that intrigued conversation for the boys. They had a lot of questions, and he answered them so effortlessly. They made him feel comfortable as they talked to him with all their slang. Shannon didn't mean to pull him away, but it was time to meet the adults. It left an awkwardness for Shannon to led Mike out of the room. Shannon started talking to Mike in a lower tone as they walked down the hall and the steps. Mike kept trying to hit Shannon's butt as he admired that she was getting a little thicker.

She remarked, "That good cooking from them hands in the kitchen is helping me to develop into my womanhood."

He laughed and said, "You're eating all your rice and cabbage… Oh yeah and bread."

She laughed.

Then, he responded. "I'm just kidding. That's good. It's looking great on you."

Before she could get to the Jewels of the house, her Aunt Leslie had already told everyone, "A boy was here for Shannon."

There was another awkwardness because Shannon could feel the tension that there was a conversation forming before they entered the room.

Her Aunt said, "Oh, honey, he is handsome. Look at those muscles."

Both Shannon and Mike smiled at the compliment. "Thank you," he replied.

They asked when she got a boyfriend. Mike looked shocked to see what her answer would be. She informed them they were just friends. They made a joke stating they both were smiling a little too hard and looking at each other with passion to be "just friends."

Shannon finally had enough and said, "Hey, don't scare my guest away."

They laughed and told him to have a seat. Although she knew his tour of introduction wasn't finished, she was relieved to know she wasn't the one making him hold off. The ladies informed her he was a catch, and they were trying to see where his head was and what goals he had with Shannon. Not only did her kings protect her, but the women didn't take any mess either. During some of the awkward questions, he was left to chuckle and answer.

The conversation was quickly interrupted by the Jewels in the kitchen with the announcement that the food was ready. Shannon felt so relieved that they could finally get off his back with the drills and questions. *"He's going to leave me alone, for sure after this,"* she thought. Everyone came to the table for prayer. Shannon had planned to head downstairs to introduce to the men of the house after he met the ladies. However, the ladies and prayer time saved the day. She was dreading introducing to the fellas because of how overprotective they are. As everyone came upstairs, side conversations were ending. The family formed into a circle to hold hands and bless the food. You could see the eyes of the men trying to figure out who was the random guy at the table. Before it could become any more awkward, and they started to assume, Shannon spoke up.

"Hey, this is my friend, Mike. Mike this is the rest of my family."

They said, "Hey. What's up?" as the guys gave Mike a deep stare.

Shannon's heart was racing.

She followed with, "Can we pray? I am starving"

"Of course you are, Greedy. Even after being the taste tester," her mom said.

Shannon's Grandfather took the honors of saying grace and prayed for the family, including her friend Mike. He kept it short.

"Thank you, Heavenly Father, for bringing my family together in unity to celebrate this Resurrection Sunday. Thank you for the food in front of us, the family beside us, and the love between us. Forgive us all for the sins known and unknown through Jesus Christ we pray."

During the prayer, Jayla kept squeezing Shannon's hand. She wanted to show her something, but Shannon knew it was not good teaching to the youth if she entertained during prayer. As the prayer ended and everyone grabbed plates, Shannon asked Jayla what was wrong. Jayla wouldn't respond. Shannon was then pulled aside by Jerome asking who her friend was. She explained that he was a friend who could potentially be more someday.

"Right now, we're just friends."

He said, "Oh you like cuz?"

She said, "Yes, I do. He's cool."

Jerome didn't want her dating, so he told her Mike looked *champ,* which meant "a mess" in other words. He was finding his flaws before even really talking to him.

She replied to Jerome, "Stop hating. He's a cool guy."

He said, "Okay, but if he ever tries you, let me know."

"Will do," Shannon said.

The others made sure they judged everything from how he moved to how he talked. They even said they could tell a mile away if he had game. They had been in the game for a while to know. Of course, the other kings in her life were not too far behind. They had been listening to her conversation with Jerome. They were sizing Mike up. However, Mike couldn't tell because Shannon had made him feel so comfortable. When DeAngelo got a little moment with him, he asked Mike a few questions and informed him that Shannon was not one to hurt. She has been their princess all her life. They would hate for anyone to try to come in her life bringing false hope and hurting her. DeAngelo Mike if he was considering getting serious with Shannon, he should respect her mind, body, and soul.

"If you don't plan on being serious with her, be real with her so that she is not opening to heartbreak," DeAngelo said.

"Shannon has stood her ground. She has stressed that the friendship must continue for now until she feels it's worthy of a relationship. She didn't want to rush and then realize we were on two different pages. I have respected her every request," Mike replied.

As DeAngelo wrapped up the conversation, they agreed that Shannon deserves a lot. They shook hands, and then made their plates. DeAngelo felt Mike's vibe was okay, but of course, his guard won't be down that easy. He didn't sense any bad vibes that raised a red flag, so he kept it respectful as he felt respected.

After seeing the way Mike eats, Shannon called him a funny eater. He is a very picky eater, but he is a grown man. He didn't eat a variety of things, but he ate a lot of what he liked. He had three hot dogs, corn on the cob, and a small piece of fish.

Shannon said, "There's rice, sweet potatoes, ham, greens, potatoes salad, and much more, and that's all you're eating?"

He laughed and said, "Yeah, I don't eat a lot of that stuff."

He didn't even like mustard or anything. He only ate a hot dog with ketchup. They laughed about it and sat off by themselves. Shannon loved getting to know the small details of him that most may not know. Surprisingly, the small conversation about the food led them to deep conversation about friendships, family, and even past relationships. Shannon was big on being able to communicate about anything, so for him to keep up made her like him even more. *To be friends with someone you must have something to talk about,"* she thought.

As Mike took a sip of his drink, he told Shannon, "You have a beautiful family. Although we are taking things slow, I do appreciate that you felt comfortable enough to bring me around."

She smiled and said, "Speaking of taking things slow. I know I stressed that to you, but I am interested in seeing where things could go."

He smiled and said, "Where did this come from?"

That reaction left her feeling that this is a possible rejection. She paused for a second not sure how to respond. He asked her a month ago to be his girl, and she asked for friendship first. She felt maybe now he wasn't ready.

Shannon was not good at hiding her feelings, and her facial expressions gave it away.

A soft voice interrupted their conversation, "Shannon, your phone has been ringing."

As her younger cousin handed her the phone, she saw twenty-three missed calls and three texts from her best friend, Riann. Shannon thanked her younger cousin and tuned into her phone. She called Riann back three times but heard nothing from her. She hoped that everything was okay. Shannon sat back down. Her somewhat rejection had her heart nervous, but to add that her friend called that many times bothered her. Mike looked Shannon in her eyes.

He asked, "What makes you so ready for a relationship now?"

She tried to think so she could answer him properly, but her mind was still clouded as she tried to gather her thoughts of what could be wrong with her friend. She started twirling her straight hair to the point it developed a curl. She looked away in fear.

He asked, "Will you look at me?"

She turned her head back towards him and said, "I'm sorry I was thinking."

He asked, "What shifted your mood?

She wanted to say, *"You're almost coming off as if you are rejecting me."* But she simply said, "I have multiple missed calls from my best friend which is weird based on how many times it was." She paused then said, "I'm just a little disturbed, but it's okay." She changed the subject to her and Mike. "I feel that I..."

The conversation got interrupted again by her mom asking were they going to dye eggs.

Shannon replied, "Yes, give me one moment, and I'll be in there."

As Shannon's mom left the room, she yelled towards the stairs, "Kids come on. We are getting ready to dye the eggs."

The kids were jumping for joy. Shannon gazed back into the conversation and wiped the crumb off Mike's chin. She quickly got to the point before being interrupted again.

"In this time of being your friend, I've been able to see that we have a great connection and can communicate about everything. If you were not able to communicate, this relationship would not only be boring but unhealthy as well."

Shannon felt he wouldn't be able to resolve future problems when they come up without that.

He looked at her for a second and then said, "That's true."

"I also feel that no matter what you may have felt, when my family made comments, you respected them. That also means you respected me."

Shannon had seen her friends regularly disrespected, even in general conversation, and that's not what she received from Mike.

He said, "Ohh no. I have a mother who is still walking this earth, and I would be crazy to degrade you in such a way."

Shannon smiled with the reassurance that he understands this is not a game to her.

She continued, "Loyalty is a huge role. I watch you with your loved ones. Prayerfully, you will carry that over if you decide to move forward with me."

With all of that in place, trust, happiness, and everything else will flow naturally. Above all, Mike's love for God caused her heart to be weak and fall for him. Mike smiled at Shannon longer than expected and made her blush.

She said, "What?" flirtatiously.

"Something about a woman who has a relationship with God brings out a deeper beauty," he said. "That's the one thing that I wanted to hear you say. If we don't have God as the foundation, we will not be able to flourish."

Now that they had an agreement, she said with a smile. "Well, are we together yet?"

He responded with a smile and said, "Yes."

The conversation took her emotions on a rollercoaster, but she was happy with the results. He took two more bites from his plate. Shannon's cousin made a joke about (glizzy gang), which is hormone joke men use when they talk about a man who eats a hot dog. The joke was stupid to Shannon, so she rolled her eyes and took his plate to the trash. They decided to partake in the family activities as she embraced her new love language with her new boyfriend.

Meanwhile, her phone rang again. It was Riann calling. Shannon made sure she didn't miss the call again. She answered the first ring. Riann called with a weeping voice. Shannon sat up giving her full attention.

"What's the matter?"

Riann inhaled, unable to speak from crying so hard.

Shannon left the room to ask again, "Hello? You okay, Poo?"

Her friend sniffed a few times and softly said, "No." When Shannon asked what's wrong, Riann wouldn't go into details. Shannon asked her friend to pull up to Aunt Leslie's house. It took her best friend about twenty minutes to get there. During that time of her waiting, Shannon went back to her boyfriend and the family. She pulled Mike aside to let him know that he would be surrounded by the family for a little while by himself while she went to see what's wrong with her best friend. He was okay with it.

He smiled and said, "Okay, Girlfriend."

They both laughed giving Shannon a release on her anxiety of hearing her best friend crying.

A text came to Shannon's phone from Riann. *"I am outside!"* Shannon went out quickly to see what could be wrong. Riann's face was puffy as if she cried for weeks, but she had pulled it together by the time she saw Shannon. As soon as Shannon hugged her, Riann broke down in her arms. Her cry bought tears to Shannon's eyes. She couldn't figure out what could be so wrong at this point. As Riann finally got it together, she spoke, but all Shannon heard was gun.

She said, "What? Slow down."

Riann took a deep breath and looked Shannon in the eyes.

"Shannon, I'm pregnant."

Shannon looked at her in shock. She quickly fixed her facial expression, so it wouldn't make Riann feel worse.

"When did you find out?"

Riann's face was frowning as if the tears were coming back. She wiped her eyes.

"This morning."

Shannon reassured her everything is okay and that she has support.

Riann said, "Yeah, but not from the one person I wish would support."

Shannon stayed quiet to give her the floor to vent. She started expressing that her tears are from fear of bringing a baby into this world. Her baby's daddy told her to get rid of it. She told him she previously had a cyst the size of oranges that blocked her tubes. They told her she wasn't going to be able to have children, and that devastated her for so long. The more she saw babies, the harder it became to accept. So, this was her moment to conceive and bring in her dream blessing.

"This not how I expected it to be," she said.

Tears started falling.

Shannon said, "It would be great if he were there. If not, you have so much support. So, don't stress. Let's go for a walk to clear your mind."

Before Riann could get out the car, she said her boyfriend had been yelling at her constantly and making her feel like she was the only one that was wrong. They were unprotected, and he knew she wasn't on birth control. He never wanted to use the pull-out method. Shannon became confused with the story. She couldn't understand why he was so angry. Rian continued her story by explaining that she tried to explain why she would like to keep it. He started pushing her toward the bathroom. He stuck the toothbrush down her throat to make her vomit. He told her she would starve the fetus under his watch and that she needs to get an abortion. She even asked was he helping to pay, and he told her no, and that was her body. Riann couldn't believe his response and how he was treating her. He made her feel like she was a whore he met last night.

As she continued to try to tell her story, Shannon's eyes were becoming glossy and forming tears to cry. She tried to hold back to be strong for her friend, but it was hard to hear the situation with no emotions.

Riann said, "When I told him I think I want to keep the baby because of my health, he looked at me calmly and walked over to the closet. I thought everything was okay and that he was just scared to hear the news. We both would be first-time parents. As I let my guard down thinking everything's okay, he walked over to me and pulled his gun out on me," she cried. "He told me that I had better not keep the baby."

Shannon's eyes were so big. She couldn't believe what she had just heard. God spared her best friend's life. What if he had shot her? Shannon regretfully missed so many calls from her. She couldn't help but hug her extremely tight. They had been friends since they were in elementary. Life apart isn't something either of them could imagine. As Shannon hugged her, the tears began to flow. It hurt her deeply to see that her friend was traumatized from such behavior by someone she loves.

Shannon began to ask question after question. "Are you okay? Did he do any physical damage to you?"

Riann replied, "He only grabbed me up and said get rid of it, or I'll get rid of both of you. If I have this baby, Shannon, he's going to kill me. But you know my opportunity of conceiving again is slim. It was a mistake, but I made my bed. I must lay in it."

Shannon didn't know what advice she could give. She had never experienced pregnancy nor had she ever had to make a sudden decision based on emotions. Shannon took her time trying to pick guys, and Riann used to laugh and say, "Girl, you will be an old lady with cats." Truthfully, what Riann constantly experienced was not fun, and that's what Shannon had been avoiding. Shannon's heart was racing, and her mind could barely keep up to process everything.

All she could say was, "We need to go into the house and get Aunt Karen."

She is the first lady of the church and would pray for Riann. Riann didn't want to go into the house because of all the attention, so Shannon pulled Aunt Karen aside.

Speaking softly, she said, "Aunt Karen, my best friend, Riann, is here, and she's hurting deeply. I will help her explain, but I'd rather say it in front of her and away from everyone else. If you don't mind, can you come outside and give her spiritual advice and relieve her heart with prayer?"

Aunt Karen didn't mind at all. She loves her nieces and nephews deeply and would do anything for them. After hearing the story, Aunt Karen instantly started praying and speaking in tongues. She suggested to Riann that she make a doctor's appointment ASAP. Then, she needed to decide what she wants to do. In hopes that she would keep her baby.

"If it's to start your family, do that alone. Next, get a restraining order, and he will have to stay away from you and the baby. Seek God's face and do not move off emotions. It can lead you to major depression and guilt. So, you must sit back and wait on God's voice."

Riann replied, "What if God doesn't speak?"

Aunt Karen tried to make her laugh and said, "Well, my non-spiritual opinion would say then he doesn't agree with departing from the child. So, He's taking His time to answer so you can reach too far along and can't have the abortion."

She smiled a little and said well, "I do want my baby, but I'm scared he will kill us."

During the conversation, Shannon's boyfriend called her inside the house. He told her that he would probably be leaving soon so that he can see his family as well. Shannon asked the ladies if they were okay. Aunt

Karen told her to go ahead inside and that she was there for Riann. Then, she prayed for Riann in private. Shannon stayed inside for a little while since she knew her friend was in good hands being with her aunt. While she was sitting next to her new boyfriend, he noticed she was shaking. She was having slight anxiety to the news of her friend. She couldn't help but wonder why the guy would act like that. They had been together for two years. He never was angry with what Shannon thought. He always showed her his sweet side. She just knew they would someday go off and elope. He showed himself to be a spiritually-driven, family man. But, Shannon quickly realized he hid who he had potential to be.

As the day progressed, Riann finally pulled herself together and came inside to get something to eat. No one could tell that anything was wrong. They laughed, played games, and enjoyed the festivities. Riann was so grateful to have her best friends' family around to keep her mind off the situation. A short while later, Shannon's boyfriend had to leave. Everyone said their goodbyes to him and finished the night with family fun.

A few moments later, Riann's boyfriend sent a text to her apologizing for how he acted earlier that day. He felt it was the perfect time to help her make the decision. He confessed that he is married to another woman who's in the military. His wife was home for a few weeks which was why he had been distant. The wife expressed her a desire for a family with him, which included children. That made his situation with Riann difficult. As Riann continued to read the text, her heart felt like it was beating out her chest. Her hands were shaking and sweaty, and tears filled her eyes.

Riann couldn't be more broken as she read it. She was happy to know why he had changed, but she was sad at the same time. A million questions ran through her mind. *A wife? An outside family? Children? I'm pregnant!?* She didn't agree to be a side chick, and she would hate to be labeled as one. She had no idea.

"We lived together. When would he have time to talk to her?"

She continued to fill her mind with questions. Despite what she felt, she knew that she was keeping her baby and would raise him or her to the best of her ability. Unfortunately, he had given Riann false hope. Shannon was so upset that she wanted to go after him herself. She was just happy that her friend was out of his reach.

Reminder:

When dating, you must know what you want and take your time getting to know your mate. There's no need to rush. If it's right for you, it will still be there when you're ready to commit. If you rush into love, you settle for things that are not in your requirements. Love can become very complicated if it's not handled with gentle, proper care. Guard your heart with diligence and watch their fruit of labor. Finding "the one" comes with trial and error. But, if you observe and date them before making it official, you learn so much more about them without labels.

Relationships can sometimes ruin great friendships, so make sure you pay attention to see if they need to stay in the friend zone. You will see early on if they are meant to be in your life or not. That would prevent you from wasting time. See what brings happiness to your potential mate. Sit back and watch how they act when upset. Learn the ins and outs about someone before giving your all to yet another wrong chance. People always start out showing the best version of themselves, confusing you into believing they're everything you dreamed of in a mate.

It takes hardships or simple pet peeves to throw their moods off and show you someone new. You must dig deep to see who's in front of you. The sooner you find out, the better. Save yourself from some heartbreaks. If you set standards, you set the bar for not allowing anyone to minimize your worth.

Ladies, please pay attention to signs. Red flags show themselves in small gestures. I am not saying to show "crazy" with major investigations. I'm simply saying do not be naïve to toxic behavior. If you have children or have to make decisions regarding a child, you must look out for your kids' best interest and make the best decisions. No matter how many people share their opinions or advice, no one can truly make those decisions for you.

Question:

What fulfills your happiness? What do you value most in a relationship? Why?

_____

_____

_____

_____

_____

_____

_____

_____

_____

Chapter 4

What's Your Deal-maker When Dating?

> ### Matthew 6:33
>
> *"But, seek first the kingdom of God and his righteousness, and all these things will be added to you."*

Mariah Stoney turned the pages of the calendar and checked off another big day. Her friend's wedding day was quickly approaching. She made it again to be yet another bridesmaid. She had been the bridesmaid in five different weddings. Mariah was the queen of standing in line to walk down with a man that is not hers to support her friend. She was always happy for her friends, but she just wished that her time was coming. Many of Mariah's loved ones were married or engaged. She couldn't believe how beautiful the unions were every time. She enjoyed going to her friend's house and seeing little things they do, whether it's her friend cooking, while he is washing the car or the couple laid up watching a movie. She loved seeing them playing games together being lovers and best friends. Mariah knew she could do that with a boyfriend, of course. However, just knowing you are under oath with God made it that much more special.

Mariah could not wait until she said, "I DO!" That was a fairytale dream since she was a small girl and prayed that God would allow her dream to come true. It saddened her heart every time she met a new man who had potential but turned out to be the opposite of what was portrayed in the beginning. In the middle of the relationship, as she started falling in love, God caused a detour and told Mariah "Pump your breaks." She couldn't understand why her. Why is it that hard to settle down? What could make things better? She has been through some liars, momma's boys, verbal abusers, cheaters, drug dealers, and the list continued. Mariah even talked to someone for a while until he confessed that he was HIV positive. She didn't have sex with him nor did she think he was a monster, but she respected his honesty, and he respected that she wanted something else.

Mariah's last relationship was almost the fairytale she wished for from his curly black hair and hazel eyes to his walk in Christ. That was until the stories started coming to Mariah that he was a liar. He lied to every person he met, and he burnt bridges in the process. She wanted to believe he was different or that he had changed. The more she tried to believe that he was different, she realized he would lie again about something so small.

One day, he walked to the store while she was asleep. When awakened, she stretched and said, "Baby, did you go to the store when I was sleep?"

She was hoping that he had brought her a snack back. He joined her on the couch and said, "No" with a straight face. She looked at the table, wiping her eyes. She was confused because an ice-cold soda was sitting right in front of her on the table. A black bag wasn't too far from the drink.

She asked, "When did you get this soda?" as she twisted the cap off to get a sip.

He said, "Oh, that? I got that a little earlier."

She knew the soda was not there earlier. It wasn't even in the refrigerator. He was breaking her trust by lying about his trip to the store. It seemed like he possibly did more than just a store run by the way he was acting.

"When I was asleep, right?" she asked.

He stopped her from trying to figure out his lie. He started kissing on her and trying to joke.

"I'm just playing. Yes, I went, baby."

She knew he was lying. In this case, his lie was for her good. He had gone to the store and did a little shopping for her. He had an outfit in the closet for her and a new pair of earrings. He knew that her trust was breaking, so he ended up showing her sooner than expected. Mariah's feelings were growing. So, she stayed with him thinking the feelings were mutual. As time went on, she realized he was much smoother with the lies than she thought. The deeper the relationship became, the more the lies grew. Mariah's momma always told her if a person keeps accusing, it's a great chance they may be doing wrong by you.

In this relationship, his trust issues were extreme. That was a bit awkward because he was the liar in it. Mariah wasn't allowed to talk to males in front of him. He felt it was disrespectful. When she did, he would call her name to distract the conversation. Then, he would lie and say someone was calling her phone or some fake story. Mariah became so in love that she made excuses for this foolishness.

One day, she called her boo to check on him because he was fighting a horrible cold. He said he would push forward to his interview. He sounded so down, but she loved his determination. Mariah took an early lunch so that she could take a nap. Her body was so tired from helping him all night. As she headed out on her break, her best friend FaceTime called her. Mariah didn't answer. She figured she could return the call when she woke up. The call came in again, so Mariah answered. Her best friend never said a word. She just put the camera on Mariah's boyfriend. He was walking to the store with his arm around a girl's neck. From her view, the two of them looked very flirtatious. Mariah couldn't say a word, she just cried. As he walked the girl to a car, they leaned in for a kiss. Mariah was devastated. She called him from her work phone and watched him ignore the call. Her friend walked to where he could see her.

"Say hi to your girlfriend," she said.

His eyes bulged, and he looked so scared. He wished he could explain, but he already knew he possibly lost Mariah. So, he didn't say much. He hoped he could still have a chance with the new girl.

Mariah told her best friend, "I've got to call you back."

Seeing that hurt her heart. She had to leave. His lies were different from the ones everyone told him about, but he was a liar for sure. It couldn't be clearer that his lies were growing. She didn't want to see how extreme they could get, so she asked to get off early. Her supervisor approved it. She went to his house and gathered all her things as he assisted her. He begged her not to leave him, but her headphones wouldn't let her hear what was said.

After dealing with this pain, Mariah screamed out in tears, "God, why me? Where is my king that you promised?"

She became mad at God. She felt that she wasn't chosen. No man wanted to wait for the "cookie." No one respected her. They couldn't match her expectations. She was left in deep thought. She didn't understand why God's desire wasn't matching hers. She was doing what he asked but still felt so far behind. Mariah's grandmother always asked when the wedding was coming or when would she give her some grandbabies. Her grandmother was applying so much pressure.

A month before, Alyse, Mariah's homegirl since kindergarten, told Mariah to mark her calendar. She invited Mariah to her gala. A special guest would be there. She was nervous but super excited to attend this event. To her, this event was a big deal. The idea of getting pampered and the whole set up to prepare for this event was like the practice idea for her wedding. It took her months to get her whole day and ideas of fashion to make perfect sense. She wanted to piece it all together to become her reality and no longer a dream. The way Mariah usually dress gave the impression that she was pure, like a virgin. She would usually dress in loose clothes and sweat suits that sometimes made her look like a young boy to some.

For this event, Mariah didn't want to be too revealing. Still, she wanted to look like the adult that she is. On the day of the event, she looked much different. She wore a beautiful long gown that hugged her body right in all the right places. Her curves detailed the perfect image of what the men love and the girls want. She usually wears flats and tennis shoes. This time, she wore red bottom pumps that finished her look with a bang. She grabbed her perfume and sprayed just the right amount to leave her signature with anyone she meets. She finished her outfit with her jewelry. When she looked at herself in the mirror, her smile revealed her confidence. She reached into her small makeup bag and grabbed her lipstick to give her lips a touch-up.

She had always kept her hair braided, but this time, she had her hair nicely straightened and never knew how long it was until then. Earlier that day, Mariah ran so many last-minute errands. She went to MAC and got her makeup done. As she was leaving the mall, she ran into an old guy that she liked in the past. He had paid her no mind previously. However, he did a double-take and greeted her so cheerfully as if they had a strong connection previously. As bad as she wanted to entertain him, she quickly remembered that she wasn't his type before. So, she was okay with passing up the option now.

He said, "Hey stranger."

With a fake smile, she responded, "Hi. How are you?"

He licked his lips saying, "I'm cool. You look beautiful."

How he treated her before, gave her another image. He wasn't as cute as she thought. She smiled at him.

"Thanks for the compliment."

Her body language showed she had things to do, so they kept that conversation brief.

He responded, "What's your number? I got a new phone."

Mariah knew she wasn't interested, so she told him, "I still have yours. I'll contact you. I must hurry."

As they said goodbyes, she thought, *"I'm glad that's over, he won't be hearing from me."*

While Mariah was home getting ready, her phone vibrated. Just like that, the guy from earlier had done his homework to contact her.

"Again, it was good running into you earlier."

She was confused when it came in because she had forgotten all about him. Plus, he'd said he no longer had her number.

She asked, *"Who is this?"*

He said, *"Devin. I apologize I didn't start like that, as good as you look, you were probably pulling all the men."*

Mariah didn't find humor in his joke.

She responded, *"Ha, no. I remember you told me you didn't have my number and here you are texting me."*

He took a little moment to text back, so Mariah put her phone down and continued to prepare for the night. As she headed to the event, she missed her exit twice because Devin called and disrupted her phone's navigation. She almost got frustrated and was going to head home, but then she reminded herself this was a special night. Not only was it just a gala event, but it was also her friend's birthday. Alyse had invited a lot of their old friends.

Mariah answered the phone saying, "HELLOOO" with attitude.

He asked, "Did someone upset you?"

She couldn't hold back. "Yes, you did. I didn't answer the first time. You keep calling, and I'm using my GPS," she said.

He apologized and asked, "Would you like me to call you back?"

"No. I told you from the beginning I would call you."

He got silent for a minute and said, "Yeah you are right, but I wanted you to know that I was serious about talking to you more."

Mariah was growing more irritated. "You weren't interested in me before, and I'm over entertaining you."

He laughed and said, "Cool. You weren't all that anyways to be acting stuck up."

She wanted to go off on him extremely. He was annoying her. She remembered what she started to dislike about him again at that moment. In the past, he would talk down on females, and disrespect them with an arrogant, cocky attitude. For someone to be that bitter to have to speak negatively to try to hurt someone intentionally, showed his true character. He needed help. Mariah just wasn't one of those girls that could tolerate her character being categorized with anything other than her name. As much as she wanted to address the situation, she knew she had a fun night ahead of her. She hung up on him and quickly blocked him.

Mariah finally arrived at her destination. When she entered the event, Alyse greeted her so cheerfully and amazed. No one had ever seen Mariah so dolled up. While Mariah gave Alyse her birthday card and balloons, they were talking, sharing jokes, and bringing laughter. Alyse felt a strong stare a mile away.

She calmly said to Mariah, "We got eyes at three o'clock."

A tall, light-skinned guy that stood about six feet tall with a pearly white smile and a partial gap kept staring at Mariah. As he was holding a conversation with the other guys around him, they could see he wasn't focused on them because he was looking in Mariah's direction. Alyse kept making jokes knowing Mariah had not had this type of attention in a while. With the comfort of being around her friend, the moment spent made her so happy that she was laughing way too hard. Mariah didn't want to give off crazy facial expressions or seem as if she was overly excited that he was paying her any attention. Although she hated how crazy she felt at that moment, it was easing her mind from the conversation on her phone earlier. Her demeanor also made him desire her more strongly. Some guys can be intimidated by a woman whose facial expressions give off a nonchalant look with the bad and bougie aura. Mariah was so pure and had a vibrant personality. She was goofy and always smiling and sharing good vibes. As the handsome stared from afar, her personality attracted him even more.

Alyse noticed he was getting up from his seat. She whispered, "He's coming, girl. I know it."

Butterflies swarmed into Mariah's stomach. She whispered to Alyse, "How do I look?"

"The bomb, Honey Girl."

Mariah smiled at the reassurance that she looks amazing. She was a good girl that suffered from major insecurities. All her friends were already in the dating game, and she never had the shot of getting a man. It wasn't because of her image that she didn't get anyone. Mariah is a very beautiful young lady. She had a few guys who tried to pursue her through friendships, but she was also picky. She was focused on school and work, and she didn't like people to distract her. Sometimes her turning them down gave them the impression that something was wrong with them. They assumed a lot, but truthfully, she just wasn't ready. As Mariah and Alyse quietly discussed the beautiful eye candy. That nice handsome young man finally took one last sip of his drink and gave his cup to the bartender. Then, he got the courage to walk over to Mariah.

"Hey, gorgeous. My name is Charles, and you are?"

Mariah smiled and said, "Hey... MJ."

He said, "Okay MJ. Is it okay if I know your real name?"

She chuckled and rolled her eyes in a flirtatious way and said, "MARIAHHHH."

"Well, MARIAHHHH," He joked and twisted his neck as if he was impersonating a ghetto woman. "When you walked past, you weren't going to speak... How rude and fake."

She chuckled and said, "No offense, but I didn't even recognize you."

His eyes widened with a huge smile as if he knew the conversation was going somewhere no matter how corny his lines could be. Mariah smiled back. He saw her smile, and that meant everything. A small voice from Alyse entered the conversation between the two of them.

"Get him, girl. I'll be back."

Mariah was a little caught off guard with her leaving them alone. She didn't expect her friend to leave, and she didn't know how to talk to this man. Although, it was already flowing with no effort. Seeing him in a suit and tie melted her heart. All she could think of was that was how he would look on their wedding day. She had to remind herself to slow down a little. As she walked over to the bartender, he held the train of her gown making sure no one stepped on it. She was so happy to see crab dip on the menu and a glass of wine. That struck another conversation because he hates seafood. In small conversation, he learned some of the things she likes and dislikes and vice versa. They both liked the way the conversation went, so before the night ended, or any random mishaps could ruin the moment, they exchanged numbers.

As she told her last four digits and he sent her a text to save his number, her song bellowed in the air. It was Brian McKnight's *Back at One*. Everyone in the building loved the song because they had all made their way to the dance floor. The handsome gentleman grabbed her hand, and they two-stepped as if no one was in the room. As she got a little more into the song, he grabbed her by the waist. Although he was tall, she still wrapped her arms around his neck. He stooped down a little more to her height. From that view, he could look in her eyes.

As they danced, he said, "You are so beautiful."

As much as she wanted to act like she hears these comments two million times a day, it melted her heart into her stomach. As they gazed in each other eyes smiling, Mariah thought, *"Oh God. Why is he getting close? Please do not kiss me. I'm not ready."* At the same time, she thought, *"Oh my, but you are so handsome and charming."* A million things ran through her mind. Alyse came up and danced her way with them. She somewhat saved the moment.

She said, "Hey new lovebirds. How is everything going?"

Mariah smiled and said, "This is Charles; Charles this is my friend, Alyse." They greeted each other. Then, Alyse asked Mariah if she wanted to join a few of her co-workers and friends for the after party. Mariah looked saddened. She wished she could join, but she told her manager she would work a double the next day. One of the shifts required her to work overnight. If she knew there would've been something else going on afterward, she would've turned it down to support her friend. Mariah knew she needed the money though, so she sensitively declined the invite.

Alyse understood. As the night was coming to an end, Alyse and Charles walked Mariah to her car. Alyse was that down friend that wasn't going to allow a new man to walk her friend or sister to the car without her. If anything happened to her, Alyse would be the one to hurt them first. On the drive home, Mariah played *Back at One* on repeat as she thought about the night and her new friend.

Mariah made it home and prepared for bed. As she was wrapping her hair and gathering the things she needed to shower, she received a text. *"I hope you made it in safely, beautiful. I enjoyed your company tonight."* Mariah smiled and responded with a long message. It took her ten minutes to gather all her thoughts. However, she deleted the whole thread and wrote a shorter message. After she looked at it before sending, she realized that text message was long, too. Mariah just deleted it altogether and didn't respond right away. She didn't want to seem overly excited. She took her shower, and as the love songs played, she let the water hit her while she thought about how the night went. She rubbed the soap gently on her face. Then, she used the rag to remove the soap. She felt like all her stress and pains were being moved away, too.

As she finished thoroughly showering, she heard her phone ring. It was Charles. She happened to hear the phone ringing as it was ending. So, she sent a short text: *"Sorry, I just got out of the shower. Thanks, I enjoyed the night as well."* He apologized for bothering her; he only wanted to make sure she was safe. He asked if she could call for a moment. Then, he remembered that she said she had to work a double. He didn't bother to hold her up, so he simply said, *"Never mind."* Mariah didn't mind talking to him as she applied lotion to her body. The sound of his voice gave her chills as she recalled his smile. She put on her chill clothes and got in the bed. The conversation was becoming so interesting with his questions that she hadn't realized how much time had passed.

As days, weeks, and even months went on, Mariah got to know Charles on a more intimate level. He truly intrigued her mind and captivated a deep passion within her heart Mariah couldn't keep her heart from falling deeply in love. During sports season, she started losing his attention. She couldn't wrap her mind around it because he flooded her attention at first. It was so much that she wondered why she didn't realize how special she was or why did it take for a man to have to tell her that. Nevertheless, she was enjoying the ride.

Mariah loved to talk, so her communication skills were beyond amazing especially when things didn't seem right.

She asked Charles, "What's up?"

He said, "Hey babe."

"No, like what's up with your absence? Why does it seem like you may be losing interest in me?"

He chuckled. Mariah's heart dropped. She could not believe he thought her question was funny when that was a time to be serious. She stayed quiet.

He said, "Hello?"

Mariah responded slowly, "Yes."

"I'm just making sure you were still here. I didn't lose interest in you. You are beautiful and amazing. It's just that sports mean everything to me, and this is the season I'm usually locked inside. I apologize if that's what it came off like because that's not the case at all."

Mariah felt so relieved as Charles reassured her on everything. Then, he told her, "I'll call you back soon. I'm getting ready to read my bible."

Her eyes lit up. Charles was different from the guys she grew accustomed to dating. The guys in her past relationships were content with smoking, drinking, partying, and running the streets. So, to hear the desire of his heart for God only attached her feelings even more. It was like he didn't have to say another word. She was hooked. She later explained what that meant to her. They began to read, pray, and fast together. She thought to herself, *"If this is the reason I've been turned down and didn't like the past guys, Charles was worth the wait."* It was that moment that made her feel special and as if God ordained their connection.

Reminder:

Although there were some flaws in Charles, Mariah developed patience. Despite the pains her ex-boyfriend caused her, she still left room for Charles to be human and make minor mistakes. Realistically, she endured situations that were meant to break her down, but it built her character into who she needed to be for "the one." After Mariah took on a liar and cheater, it felt impossible for her to find a man that intrigued her mind. She needed someone that could bring her peace just as Charles had done. Despite how much she yearned to be in love and married, there were things she wasn't settling for in relationships. Just as we have deal-breakers, we have deal-makers.

Before walking into a relationship, you must first allow yourself time to love on yourself. By doing this, you give yourself the opportunity to see what keeps you happy and what saddens you. If you can't find peace within, no one on earth can offer that to you. You don't find happiness in other people. Instead, you must find what's fulfilling within you and then you hold the bar for your mate to keep you happy. However, they can only fulfill your happiness momentarily. Every new relationship starts great, but when those moments get tough, you need to tap into those moments that kept you happy when you were alone. It's your safe place so that you don't lose yourself in love. Be alone sometimes, treat yourself out, and find hobbies to keep yourself occupied. Don't make a person your whole world and leave yourself no room to walk in it.

Deciding to be alone at times doesn't mean you are lonely. Someone that's added to your life should be like an accessory. It brings a nice finishing touch, but it's not the whole outfit. They give you that extra glow to sparkle as they are adding happiness to your life. Your whole world should not revolve around them so much that you can't think straight when they are away for only a moment. Most women at some point have made this mistake in life. When you put your all into someone, especially when you are not married, and they let you down, it's even harder to pick yourself back up. Keep God first and allow Him to be above all. When the time is right, you'll have confirmation.

Question:

What is your deal maker? What are the qualities you search for when looking for your soul mate?

_____

_____

_____

_____

_____

_____

_____

_____

_____

_____

Chapter 5

How to Master the Art of Composure When Falling in Love

---

1 John 4:18

"There is no fear in love, perfect love casts out fear. For fear has to do with punishment. And whoever fears has not been perfected in love."

Loud music, laughter, and talking filled the room on a Friday night at the start of girls' night. Lina was enjoying a glass of sweet white wine as she listened to nice R & B music playing. The vibe was great for her after having a long work week working overnight. Lina and her friends were gifted in many ways. Therefore, they were all able to contribute to the gathering to make it a success. Each friend picked a project to work on from the decorations to the food and DJ all the way to the activities. It was a night to detox from anything they may have faced. No one had to face their problems alone.

Because everyone was close-knit, they were able to share some of their stress and receive great encouragement and advice from each other. Aside from health or elderly family members to keep in prayer, the biggest topic was about relationships, of course. Lina had gotten her heartbroken deeply a year and eight months ago. That pain was hurting her so badly that she thought she would never become open like that again. If any men approached her, she simply would tell them, "I do not do relationships."

Although, some guys didn't ease up from a response like that. However, she was one that meant what she said and stuck by it no matter what. At one point, she had eye candy, but then she realized that he was a major drug dealer. She was tired of being attracted to the dope boys.

Lina worked a full-time job overnight and a part-time job a few hours during the day. Although her friends told her to slow down, her ambition allowed her to work her side hustle of doing lashes, too. She understood why they said slow down and enjoy life, but she also knew that she wanted her future to be set. She didn't want to live in a small apartment anymore, so she had to hustle to live her best life and support her loved ones. In the beginning, missing holidays and certain events made her want to relax a bit, but she adapted. Being busy became her life. If she slowed down, she would feel like something was missing.

Lina was running from pain, so staying positively busy allowed her to not deal with it. She kept herself so busy that she didn't leave room to get acquainted with anyone. She didn't even have time to spend with the ones she did know. As Lina sat and enjoyed a nice drink and soft music, her homegirl, Paris, knocked three times on the door. As Lina asked, "Who is it?" her smile grew so big to greet her friend. They hadn't seen each other in a few years. Paris's hands were full of games for the girls to play. As Lina took the game into the living room and assisted Paris with getting settled, she noticed that the DJ for the night, which is their friend Taija, and Paris didn't speak to each other.

Lina backtracked and said, "No bad vibes," and looked at them both.

Paris jokingly said, "Girl, I was going to speak. I had to put everything down."

They both knew she was lying! Taija got caught last year at the gas station with Paris's ex, and that caused them a fallout. Paris never took the time to ask any questions. The ex-boyfriend was off limits. It's against the code, so she felt betrayed.

Before the guests arrived, Lina said, "Let's kill the bad tension."

Lina did most of the talking for them.

"Paris, I understand why you were upset. Trust me; I get it. However, nothing inappropriate was going on between the two. Taija caught a flat tire on her way home, and your ex-boyfriend was at the same location. When he noticed that she looked troubled, he asked what was wrong, and she explained. Your ex-boyfriend had his friend help him change Taija's tire. When Taija asked how much he was expecting her to pay for his service, your ex-boyfriend told her she will always be family, so no worries.

"As he finished up with her tire, Taija noticed the boys were walking. She yelled out that she could give them a ride. That was the least she could do. His friend declined the offer because his girlfriend was meeting him with his car at a location down the street. The friend lived thirty minutes away. Instead of the friend driving your ex-boyfriend home, your ex-boyfriend felt it would be easier for Taija to do it. So, she did. She didn't know she would have to consult with you about it since it was innocent. Before she took him home, she stopped at the gas station where she saw you. Who knows, Paris? She probably would've told you the story, but we will never know.

"Again, I understand your frustration. But life is way too short to be beefing over a misunderstanding. I don't understand why as women, we give chance after chance to these dead-beat fathers and disrespectful

BOYfriends, but we're quick to cut a friend off for minor mistakes or Misunderstandings. Your friend is more solid than that man you constantly keeping around. Nah, she can't fulfill you sexually, but mentally, spiritually, and emotionally, your friend is more understanding in the end. Cut the beef as of today, if not for yourself, for me."

Without Paris asking Taija what she was doing with her ex-boyfriend, she instantly went off. She was ready to attack Taijia, but he stood in the middle and didn't allow it to get that far. The night became full of arguments and name calling. Since that day, Paris and Taija avoided each other. However, Lina needed all her girls in this season of her life. She requested that they put their differences aside to fulfill a great night. Lina was so busy in her world that she had forgotten about the incident. As she finished explaining her view heart to heart, Paris told her she already knew the story.

Lina responded, "What? So, why are you still upset?"

Paris explained that when they departed from the gas station, she still had access to her ex's things. Later that night, she saw the messages between Taija and him. He asked if she made it home safely. Taija responded that she did. He apologized that she had to go through that. Taija said, *"Yea me too. That's my girl. I don't know why she would think I would stoop that low. I understand it looked bad, but she didn't even let me explain.*

He said, *"It's okay. Try not to worry. She would always tell me what's done in the dark will always comes to light."*

Her ex-boyfriend was right. Paris was being nosy and got answers. She admitted that she was too prideful to reach out because of the way things ended. Lina responded, "You were not wrong for how you felt. However, you were wrong on how you handled it. Paris was grown enough to admit her wrongs and apologize."

Lina smiled and said, "Aww, Pumpkin, you are growing up."

Paris and Taija laughed.

As they smiled, Taija asked, "Can I get a hug?"

Paris ran over to hug Taija. Meanwhile, the door opened slowly. Lina couldn't believe she accidentally left the door open. The guest had knocked, but the ladies didn't hear it because they had been deep in conversation with the music playing. Luckily it was Kylie, Lina's next-door neighbor who she developed a nice relationship with over time. Lina welcomed her with open arms and introduced her to the other ladies.

When fuel is flaming within her circle, Lina feels obligated to step in to keep her circle close. They are her family. She is that friend that brings peace to your situation. Mentally and spiritually, she has special words of encouragement to help you see beyond your faults. Truthfully, it's like God touches her and uses her to speak for Him at times, and she doesn't even notice. Her advice would bring tears to all of her friends' faces at some point in their friendship. She would speak to their hearts and souls without them even asking because of how much she cares for them. It's like she grew a deep bond full of passion that allows her to look at them and know when something wasn't right with them.

If she talked long enough, she could go around the room and give a message to each of them. At times, they didn't fully explain their pain. Although she hadn't gone through as much, her words would often just wow them.

She never judged, made them feel bad, or belittled their emotions. Lina felt it was a gift and a curse to have that passion. Sometimes, they would abuse the advice by going days and weeks without calling her and forgetting that she faces pain, too. When they did call, she would smile ear to ear excited only to see that they were calling for yet more advice. Sometimes, it could be challenging for her because no matter what she was doing, busy or not, if that phone rang and she heard tears, she dropped what she was doing. She had a hard time saying no. She also battled how extreme a situation could become if she wasn't there. She worried that the guilt of her not being there would trouble her. However, she was suffering in her skin, too.

This girls' night had been planned for some time. It was a night to clear their minds from everything that they may face in their personal lives. As the girls were enjoying the music and sharing laughs, Lina was in the kitchen finishing up her famous taco sauce for the chips. *"Mmm tasty,"* she thought as she dipped the fork in the pan to have a taste. Meanwhile, the other ladies began to arrive. They all fixed their plates and prepared to start playing games. They played a game called *Dirty Minds.* Lina passed out blank paper and pens and said that she would describe things and they must guess it.

She used an example: "What goes in your mouth that's liquid and white? When you finish, you spit."

Of course, their good girlfriend Shawny said, "I'm a freak because what I thi--."

Lina cut her off with a laugh and said "Write it down. I guess we will see in the end."

They finished all twenty questions full of laughter. They were so excited to see if their answers were correct and what the others thought it could be. They were laughing so hard when realizing their minds were so dirty! Just spending time with each other made it more exciting. Lina informed the girls that the answer to the example was toothpaste. They laughed and joked for some time when they realized how wrong a lot of their answers were.

Shawny said, "Man, maybe the freak in me misses Lorenzo."

Paris told her; girl, "Tonight, go home and get your mind on these jokes."

She made a sad face and said, "We aren't together."

The other girls had no idea they were separated.

"Wait, didn't he just propose? Oh my. I'm sorry to hear that," Paris said.

Lina went to comfort Shawny.

Shawny said, "It's okay. Things happen, right? Once a cheater always a cheater."

Everyone was shocked to hear those words. They couldn't believe Lo would mess that up again. Shawny had her crazy ways, but she treated that man with so much love and respect. Lina knew something wasn't right about him. In fact, she asked Shawny was she sure that she was ready. She never told her to leave, but she did tell her to watch closely and to make sure she protected her heart. When Lina told Shawny that, she was too head over hills and admiring the gifts he bought that she didn't even realize the red flags. She kept saying to Lina, "Girl, he changed. I am guarding my heart with diligence. I'm going to make him work for this." But, in a matter of hours, he was back in her bed where he knew he could capture her heart and soul every time. He found her weakness and abused it. She kept talking tough, but her actions made her weaker by the day until she felt she couldn't live life without him.

The girls allowed her to express her pain. Then, they gave her their opinions and advice. They held each other up while also holding each other accountable for their shortcomings. They were not bashing or judging each other. They simply said what they could do the next time differently. Nevertheless, it was easy to have the vision to see what someone else couldn't when you are on the outside looking in. Sometimes their flesh and desires screamed in their ear louder.

Lina was the queen of advice, which is what Shawny couldn't wait to hear. It was easy for her because her emotions weren't caught up blinding her perspective of certain men in the relationship. She wasn't damaged, so she didn't speak from bitterness. As a mother to a child, her love was so deep that she always wanted to make sure people surrounding her friends were good for them. She had instincts as well. Being this involved with her friendships sometimes caused her stress. What they didn't realize was that her love for them was beyond skin deep. Therefore, when they were hurt, she would be hurt, too. She honored their love and presence, and she was glad to be their go-to person. She used to say, "When I find a man, I don't know how you will feel, but that day will soon come." She often wondered if they would be there for her if she needed them. She wouldn't find out until she took a leap and started to date.

Lina prayed specifically on the guy that she wanted to marry. She wrote her prayer in a journal and prayed for the physical, mental, and spiritual sides of her spouse. For a long time, she turned down many men because they weren't what she asked for in her husband. She was very picky and protective of her heart. She had a strong fear that she battled because of her friends' relationship stories and how crazy their significant others made them look. She never wanted to have to go through such a thing. Sometimes it wasn't always the fault of who they were in relations with, because it was sometimes her friends that allowed it. Furthermore, they would continue to go back to the men after they had hurt them.

Some of the guys even began to dislike Lina because she had been on the other end of the phone when her friends would vent. So, in the eyes of the boyfriend, Lina was the bad guy who made trouble. She didn't care what their significant other thought or felt about her having friends' backs. She was a real friend by listening in their time of need. If they ever asked for Lina advice, she gave it. Lina never cared to be in anyone's business. However, if they opened the door for her to enter, she would take a seat only to listen unless asked for her input.

When the friendships became disrupted, it would be because some friends would be so in love that they had no voice to defend Lina when their men assumed that she could be giving information instead of simply listening. When the couple would get back on good terms, some friends would distance themselves from Lina to pacify the boyfriend. That wasn't fair to Lina because she was only being a friend supporting her friends in need. Unfortunately, when things got bad in their relationships, they cried on Lina's shoulder again. No matter how fake that felt to Lina, her heart would never allow her to close them out. The sad thing is that Lina was rooting for love and pushing for happiness in whichever form they perceived it. She never said to leave or stay. Her motto was: "If you are safe and not being abused, then follow your heart."

Lina waited a very long time for her prince. She was very particular in what she wanted until one day she learned that what she may desire in a man may not be God's plan. It was hard to accept that idea, but it made perfect sense to her. So, she started trying to mellow her standards to be a little more realistic. It was hard because as soon as the guys slipped up, she became uninterested. She met this one guy named Nathaniel. She found the qualities she had prayed for and accepted the ones she didn't. After spending time together and learning so much about each other, Lina felt herself falling for him.

On May 12, 2010, she set aside her nerves and boldly said, "Look, you're mine."

Her mind was racing, unsure of what he would say in response. She was trying to figure out if she said it too aggressively or if she didn't say enough. She couldn't tell if she was rushing things or if he would be ready, too. Her fear of rejection became stronger at that moment.

He gently responded, "You're mine, too." Although she was happy, she was very nervous about the new relationship. She had never given anyone the time of day, and he was the lucky guy. Lina remembered every bad phone call her friends had with their male friends. That made her fear even wanting to start a relationship. Naturally, it was a little discouraging for someone who seen and read all positive things about love yet everyone around her was having a tough time figuring it out. She had a strong fear, and in that season, he was very patient with her. She didn't give her all because she was taught, "Don't put all your eggs in one basket." With fear, it made perfect sense to follow that advice.

Early one Sunday morning, Lina was blasting gospel music while preparing for church. Some of the gospel music moved her spirit. She couldn't help but shed a tear. She knew that it was an amazing feeling that felt surreal, but she felt numerous emotions towards it. The whole ride to church, she constantly wondered if she could finally be in the right space or if it was the enemy in disguise. When she got to church, the word was speaking on faith. At this point, she believed her boyfriend was the guy she had prayed for over the years.

 Lina had started to love everything about him from his beautiful smile to his slim body frame, and most of all how he grabbed her attention most by intriguing her mind. When she would see him, it made her heart skip beats. As he reached to touch her, the chills on her body became noticeable. When he kissed her, she felt like she wasn't here on earth. He had her heart, and she couldn't control it. She was able to see that "in-love filling" that everyone talked about and yearned for in their lives. She loved him through the high winds and stormy nights to his stinky body sweat after a long hot scorching day. She loved him so deeply that his flaws were now unnoticeable. In her eyes, he was a perfect piece that everyone probably wished to have.

 Nathaniel would do small things that made her blush. After a long day from class or work, he would have her favorite snacks available for her when she went to visit him. As she would sit watching T.V., he would be mesmerized as he adored her appearance. He could never keep his hands off her, so she often received massages from him. If she vented about a bad day, he would have some surprise up his sleeve to cheer her up. Nathaniel always called in to check on her wellbeing and to make sure she found time to eat and drink water.

People told her he was a bad boy. They tried to tell her to be careful because he doesn't stay true to himself. She heard negative statement after negative statement. His ex-girlfriends would tell her he was a cheater. They would make fake social media accounts and phone numbers to harass her about the relationship. *Being in a relationship that's publicly known is hard,* she thought. However, being secretive to hide their love wasn't an option. She was so happy about that.

If anyone ever told her negative about the relationship or how he felt about her, his actions would prove them wrong every time. He would express his gratitude for her in multiple ways. Just as much as he spoiled her with love, Lina took care of her man by completing all her girlfriend duties. Sometimes she went to the extreme by completing wifely duties for him. For certain, she made sure her man was satisfied to keep him doing the things he did for her. She was unbothered with all the negativity because his past didn't define who he grew to be. Every man will change at some point and for the right person. She was never a saint in her past, so if that discouraged him from wanting to pursue her, he could miss out on the woman she was. She was amazing, and everyone who met her said it. So, she allowed him the chance to show his change.

As time progressed, they became the relationship goals for many. Lina didn't like being put on that pedestal because she knew they were human, and things could shift in the blink of an eye. However, she was that much in love that she didn't mind powerfully showing her love. They gave many hopes, especially her friends who were suffering from toxic love. She gave them a visual of what love should be. Their love was like an intense feeling of deep affection. They didn't fall for each other's material belongings. They weren't just in love with physical appearance, money, fashion, or vehicles. They built their connection directly from the heart. Lina was able to tell him things she could never speak on to anyone else. She had done some things she said she'd never do, and she had patience through every storm that even left tragic aftermaths.

"Patience is endurance under difficult circumstances."

During the difficult moments, she learned to be patient by understanding that two people with two different backgrounds were coming together as one. He would say to her, "Ayyyyeee, my baby is amazing. She is going ride with me through whatever, and I'll hold her down FOREVER!" Although he often reminded her of that quote, she was still afraid. She didn't want to become so vulnerable by giving her whole heart to him while being unsure if he could manage the pressure of staying faithful and committed.

She often asked herself, *"If we're growing, why are we so afraid now?"* She was afraid to be so into him that she seemed desperate and would be mistaken as obsessed. She was also afraid that his listening ears would become muted, and he would stop communicating. She thought the agreement was to build. However, she wondered what if the efforts stopped after he got her. She had never been in love before, so her fears were from what she had seen and heard. Nevertheless, he was different, and every time she got worried, he reassured her that she was safe in his arms.

Reminder:

In every situation, a chance or risk is taken before the actions occurred. That is not saying do things you know aren't right. It's simply saying to take the chance of loving someone. Lina had experienced negative examples of what love looks like in her generation. Those examples left her to believe she would never love or be loved as her heart desired. There's a possibility you may not get the love language right on the first try. You may get hurt. However, you will build character, understanding, and more value when you pick yourself up after the heartbreak. No, heartbreaks are not fun. No, that doesn't mean settle because you expect heartbreak after heartbreak. No, it doesn't mean that people will not talk down on the decisions you make.

You must take risks and believe that God ordained everything we face in life for a reason. Taking a risk can also give you the equal possibility that you will find your soulmate on the first try. It's a possibility that you'll find the one who's already finished playing games and was brought up with a great background. Most importantly, make sure you are evenly yoked as the Bible makes clear. You must take time to truly trust in God with your heart, even as small as a pinch of salt or a tiny mustard seed.

Understand that even when you go through something, if it's not God's will, it may hurt to break free. However, He will end it. He doesn't want His babies staying in bondage. God will line up something better. Just trust Him. When you are dating, watch the fruit of their labor. Pay attention to red flags. Don't be the Negative Nancy looking for trouble but be alert. No matter how many love stories you've read, movies you've seen, or friends that have only shared the good, you will go through things in a relationship as you will in life. Period. There's no dodging that.

If life went perfectly, what would be our purpose? Take a chance and trust the process. God is working overtime to make sure you are happy and ready for your soulmate when you meet him. If you live in fear and decide not to try, you will never know what God has for you. You will receive bumps and bruises along the way, but it will mature you, mold you, and build you to be the right person for whomever God has for you!

Question:

What is your fear in dating and why?

_____
_____
_____
_____
_____
_____
_____
_____
_____
_____
_____
_____
_____
_____
_____
_____
_____

Chapter 6

What's Your Deal-breaker While Searching for a Long-term Commitment?

Galatians 6:7

Do not be deceived, God is not mocked; for whatever a man sows, this he will also reap

---

"Ouch! Oh my. What could be wrong now? What looks like the best thing, can be a silent killer!" Shawna McKinley thought. Have you ever craved a food dish because a picture of it looked so appetizing? Maybe you drove an extra twenty minutes to get it and even bought the biggest platter only to find out it wasn't the taste expected. Well, Shawna based her relationships on that experience. She felt she must sample things and men to see if they were worth the money, time, and effort.

Shawna was very beautiful, strong, and self-driven. She had been through so much in her life that she had no tolerance for games. During the first dating phases, she learned that a person would praise themselves to be the one you are looking to date. They would go the extreme by lying to tweak the spark within themselves! A few dates later, it's your job to analyze and observe to see the lies from the truth. Shawna learned this quickly. She had experienced the "momma's boy" who couldn't make decisions on his own. She dated the "insecure boy" who couldn't handle her chasing her dreams because it took too much time away from him. She experienced the "control freak" who couldn't stand her making decisions without communicating with him. She babysat the "crybaby" who complained every chance he could. She dealt with the boy who felt he wasn't the man unless he had more than one female. She even dated the shopaholic, fake rapper, club promoter, and others. Shawna felt boys were a fraud with many similarities that she couldn't deal with in a relationship. So, for a long time, she chose to stay away.

Finally, she experienced a good guy that everyone loves. He seemed to be well put together. Shawna knew the games before they could even prepare to be played, so she didn't see any red flags with this guy. Her family and friends always wanted him around. He was the cool guy that had an amazing personality and a charming demeanor. They also loved how he treated Shawna. He looked at her as if no one else was in the same room. His love for her was too sweet at times that it didn't seem real. Shawna would ask for everyone's opinion about him to make sure she wasn't overlooking something. However, surprisingly, no one came up with anything negative. NO ONE!

He was the affectionate type. He couldn't keep his hands off Shawna, and it wasn't sexually. He just loved her so much that he craved her affection, attention, and time. He could go without everything else. If he could be around her, he was completely satisfied. The relationship was different from what she was used to in the past. Guys would lust behind her, but they never gave the impression that they couldn't go a second without her. As much as Shawna hated the way her feelings were developing, he made her heart smile. His jokes not only brought a smile to her face, but anyone who met him enjoyed his presence.

On July 4th, as the fireworks lit so brightly and beautifully in the sky, her heart was filled with butterflies. Behind her stood a handsome young man that held her with a grip of protection and a scent so soft but strong enough to smell. When she looked at him, his smile was the icing to her cake. Something about his presence made her feel complete. However, she still decided to take things very slowly. She sometimes avoided making eye contact with him because she didn't want to become weak and vulnerable. They smiled as the many colors filled the sky. When the heart-shaped fireworks illuminated the dark canvas, they tried to capture themselves in front of the beautiful scene with kisses, hugs, and smiles. The night was so beautiful and romantic. They both loved it. The fireworks were coming to an end, so they wrapped their things up and made their rounds to say goodbye to her family.

When they got in the car to leave the fireworks show, he looked in her eyes with a slight smile and said, "Baby, you are so special to me. I love you at the same level as I love my mom, and that's deep... That's real. If I lost you today, I would want God to take me too because I couldn't do life without you."

Shawna knew he felt so strongly about his mom. Their relationship was amazingly close. As she looked at him and let his words marinate, her mind said, *"Girl, stop him now. That's way too deep,"* but her heartfelt his words to the core. She had never heard that one before. He spoke so smoothly and passionately. It wasn't words in writing or something he had copied and paste. It was straight from his mouth into her heart. As sweet as that was to her, she tried to act like a tough soldier. She still gave the side eye because she knows the game, and it was almost as if he was running one on her. She looked away, he kissed her cheek, and they drove off.

As months passed, they became more serious as they allowed the relationship to flow. He introduced her to his family, and she got more involved in his personal life. Although she was still guarded as she continued to learn who he was, she began to let her guard down a little after meeting his family. They had great stories about him, and they loved him dearly. In fact, after hearing a few stories of his childhood, Shawna realized they had so many similar situations that they faced in their lives. Being open about their treasures that few would know helped them understand and connect on a deeper level.

Life had become complete for Shawna with him in her life. They had been dating, traveling, and loving extremely hard. They decided to take a cruise and get away. The cruise ship was equipped with a pool, golf course, basketball court, game night, casino, and more. It was their first experience, and they were enjoying every second of it. As the night came, and they sat on the rooftop enjoying the breeze and listening to the waves, they decided to talk. They shared their future dream and goals, and the deeper the conversation got, the more they were falling for one another. The night wasn't over, so they partied and enjoyed each second, they spent together. Later that night around 3:00 a.m., Shawna grabbed her mouth and ran to the bathroom to puke. The boat rocking was becoming too extreme. Her boo heard her and came towards the bathroom.

"Are you okay?" he asked.

"Ye…"

Here comes the puke again. She wanted to say she was okay, but she felt horrible. Tears started falling because all she wanted to do was enjoy the trip. Her boo went to grab her something to drink and to get her a seasickness patch from the front desk. As they went back to sleep, she began to feel better, and she was able to finish the trip with fun. About three weeks after the trip, her boo started becoming clingy. Shawna didn't mind because he gave her a sense of peace when he was around. While in the comfort of her bed, she got up running to the bathroom to puke again.

"What the hell is wrong with me?" she said.

Shawna knew something wasn't right, so she called up her doctor to make an appointment. They told her not to wait and that she should come in right away. She hung the phone up and laid there for a few minutes hoping that the butterfly feeling in her stomach would stop. Then, she got up and ran a nice, hot shower. She entered the water very slowly. It seemed the heat was helping a lot. When she got out of the shower, she put on some comfortable clothes and headed to see the doctor.

When she arrived at the doctor's office, the nurse immediately took her to the back and hooked her up to an I.V. She had been dehydrated. While she was resting, her arm bent like a Charly horse had locked it up, and she couldn't control it. She cried and screamed because of the pain it caused her. Before the medical staff could give her anything for the pain, they made her urinate. They also drew blood and tested her for everything. While the doctor ran tests, she called her boo over fifteen times, but he wasn't answering. She was becoming worried because it wasn't like him. As she began to grow frustrated by hearing the voicemail again, the doctor knocked softly and entered. She had a weird look on her face.

"Ms. Johnson, you are pregnant," she said.

Shawna's eyes bulged in surprise.

"Wait, what?"

She couldn't believe her ears. She didn't know what to feel except fear of relaying that message to her boo. Finally, he called back. Before she could tell him the details of the visit, he rushed over to the doctor's office. That's where she delivered the message. He was happy. He kept saying, "I hope it's a boy." Shawna was afraid of becoming a mom, but the excitement that filled his voice put her feelings at ease. The doctor told her she was dehydrated and needed to rest. She also needed to slow down a little to avoid early miscarriage. She agreed to follow the doctor's order as she was released.

Later that month, Shawna met a friend of her boo's mom. They were in a store, and she recognized Shawna. Shawna didn't know who this stranger was walking up on her, but she kept a smile on her face. The lady started expressing things from her boo's past, and she exposed information about him. Some of it was about him being in the streets doing things that could come back to haunt them. She went on to say that he has a baby that he doesn't deal with or claim. Shawna wasn't trying to accept that because it sounded like the information came from bitterness or jealousy. However, she was still mindful that this could be a moment of red flags to heed.

As the friendship turned into a relationship, Shawna started to notice some things. He had been a liar, and that's something she had dealt with before. She had ex-boyfriends who lied to cheat or said they'd be home by ten but came home at 4:00 a.m. However, her boo was a liar on another level. He lied about the big things like his source of income all the way to the small things like his outfit down to his socks. Nevertheless, Shawna's feelings had grown so extreme that she tried to give him a chance. He wanted her to understand that he liked her and wanted her to believe he had the potential to be everything great. He had failed to realize that she would have accepted him no matter his storms because she had been in storms as well.

She still couldn't believe the woman at the store had told her the truth. He was the sweetest guy she had ever met. On top of that, she was pregnant with his child. Shawna didn't make eye contact for personal reasons. Now, she regretted that because she learned that the eyes would've shown her the lies early in the relationship. She was furious with him because God suddenly started revealing different things day after day. Every lie was coming out, and it was getting worse and worse. At this point, there was no room to work on the relationship because it was pretty much a lie as well. It got so extreme that he tried to protect the lies and character he created so much that his frustration allowed him to disrespect her. He even called her disrespectful names.

His character was beginning to change, and that was hurting Shawna more than the lies. He got so mad at the threat of her leaving that he told her she was only for sex with the next man because that's all they wanted from her. He was trying to manipulate her to believe no one would love her as he did. He also kept telling her that she wouldn't leave him because she was carrying his baby. Honestly, her heart wanted to stay, but her mind was made up. That wasn't love that she was experiencing with him. If it had been love, he would have been able to look her in the eyes with an honest tongue no matter how painful the situations were. He was lying about things that didn't even concern her. She hadn't even asked him about some of the things he lied about to her. He just came out with stories and lies which just made it worse.

Shawna was a workaholic. Although he also worked, he didn't work as hard as she did. Therefore, he couldn't understand her ambition. He told her she had to enjoy life as much as she worked, and she agreed. As a result, she became distracted by fun, and she began to slack on things she needed to get done. He took a lot of her time and her attention, so moving forward to get back on track became stressful. However, she needed to get her life back in order, and that's what she planned to do. As she was gathering her things to leave, he continued with the harsh words.

"All you know is money, huh?"

He was trying every way possible to make her seem like the bad person.

She replied, "The same way I made you fall in love without sex, I can make the next man fall in love, too. That comes with being honest, real, and most of all, being a woman. I'm not anything that you have called me, but I thank you for that because I no longer feel bad for making my decision. Your lies have now been revealed."

He couldn't handle the feeling of rejection, but he caused this upon himself. Shawna was so confused, but she found this to be hilarious. She thought, *"How did I let him slip through the cracks?"* It didn't matter why or how. Walking away with her dignity and self-check was the best feeling in the world especially knowing that she left behind her mark. When he tries to bad mouth or blame her for their breakup as he did a girl from his past, the truth will reveal because habits don't break overnight. No matter how much he would say he didn't care, she struck a nerve by just being herself.

Sometimes major experiences can change into new results. Hopefully, he learned from that relationship and another female won't have to deal with his negative behaviors. Even if he had come clean with all his lies, the trust was damaged. He had degraded her as a woman, and God's word says the power is in the tongue. His tongue had the power to end their relationship.

Shawna held her head high and walked with confidence without looking back. Her eyes were full of tears, but she was determined to make it to her car without him noticing her sadness. She didn't want to show any weakness. As she drove off, her phone rung. It was him calling, so she ignored it. Eight calls later, she decided to put her phone on silent. She made her way to a friend's house. Shawna never went there while they were dating, so it was a great place to avoid him knowing where she was. After calling her friend to let her know she was outside, she saw that she had thirty-two missed calls and ten text messages from him. He kept apologizing. The last message read:

"You were right, Shawna. What I told you on how I felt, I meant. That was not a lie. When I told you I want my son, that was not a lie. When I opened to you about things that concerned me or troubled me, that was not a lie. I felt it was too soon to share some of those things with you not knowing how you would look at me. I wanted to tell you, but after I knew you loved me how I love you, I felt it would devastate you as it has done. I don't mean to hurt you, and I made a mistake by calling you those names. You know you are beautiful and special, Shawna.

"Man, I lost you. I lost my family because of Karen. She always has been messy, and it's sad. It's not all her fault. It's not her fault at all because I should've told you. She was wrong though. her motive was to break us, and

*you didn't deserve to find out from anyone else but me. Yes,
I made mistakes in my past. As you've always said, it
doesn't define me. I wish I had told you sooner. I wish we
could restart. I'm asking for yet another chance and having
my family back. I'm stupid, man."*

Shawna went inside her friend's house and instantly
broke down in tears. While crying, she felt like she was
peeing on herself. Shawna ran to the bathroom to see a
huge spot of blood. As she sat on the toilet, it was
confirmed that in that very moment that she was
miscarrying her child. *How could he have destroyed my life
breaking every ounce of me?* She wasn't happy to lose her
kid. She was torn. However, she was relieved to know that
the baby wouldn't have to suffer from the brokenness of
another damaged home.

Reminder:

I conducted a small survey amongst my peers, and
I've heard all types of deal breakers. They were things such
as bad breath, ugly shoes, bad fashion, no money, no car,
living home with parents, terrible sex, and more. There is
no right or wrong answer to a deal breaker. We all have
preferences when dating, and that's why there is someone
for everyone. As I reviewed all the survey answers, I
noticed something. The deal breakers listed were either
material or physical. Let's reevaluate this.

In the next five years, everything listed above plus
the ones I didn't list are all fixable. A person can find a job
that may even pay more than your salary. A quick dental
visit can straighten teeth and catch that infected tooth that's

causing bad breath. With that new money, they can purchase a new wardrobe, car, and even own a home.

I'm not asking or telling you to lower your standards. I'm telling you to take some time to evaluate what satisfies your happiness and what disrupts your frustration when dating. Jot down your answers this is how you can start specifically asking God for your queen or king to enter your life. After being through some things in the love department, I realized my huge deal breaker that grinds my gear. The one thing that will make me chop you off quick is a liar! Yes, that can be worked on as well. What if the trust is broken before we can even commit to a relationship? Lying is hard to do because of all the stories you have to keep up in line. The more you get away with it, the more you start to make a habit of lying. Shawna endured so much pain from a liar and couldn't believe how long she had him around before his lies were revealed. Nonetheless, her lustful desires muted the red flags. He learned what fluttered her heart and used it to manipulate her. He was a liar!

I've learned that we can create and stop our storms through our use of free will. Some people see the blessings upon you and have motives. They are looking at you and plotting on your demise. How could they have such cruel mindsets? What's even sadder that some of the liars are more into religious backgrounds, but they are the most envious. The same way God sends people to help you, the enemy sends people to distract and break you. This is all ordained by God so that you can build within your character. Watch the fruit of the labor surrounding you and make your best judgment. God gives us intuition. I like to refer to it as a silent voice from God. Never allow yourself to ignore your intuition because it's a message informing you when it is time to make a shift in your life and cut folks off. Be obedient and do so. In the dating phase, try not to be so judgmental. However, still be mindful and observe who's entering your life, especially when kids are involved. If Shawna had had her baby, the things her child would have dealt with would've broken Shawna. She was beyond hurt to have to lose her lover and her baby all in one day, but she knew that God would help her through it.

My heart goes out to all the parents who have had an abortion, ectopic pregnancy, miscarriage, stillborn, or have had to bury a child. No matter how it happened, when it happened, or what happened, the pain endured physically, mentally, and emotionally is real. Going from loving someone so deeply and calling an end to their life is hard to deal with at any time. I could never tell you what not to feel because your feelings belong to you. What I can say is never give up on yourself or your life. Allow yourself time to grieve. But, get back up because your life is still precious. There's purpose in all your process. Trust God to direct you through. It's not over until God says so.

Question:

What is a deal breaker for you, and why?

_____

_____

_____

_____

_____

_____

_____

_____
_____
_____
_____
_____
_____
_____
_____
_____
_____

How can you tell if someone isn't the one?

_____
_____
_____
_____
_____
_____
_____
_____
_____
_____
_____
_____
_____
_____
_____
_____
_____

Chapter 7

Am I Lusting or Loving?

Galatians 5:22-23

"But the fruit of the Spirit is love, joy, peace, forbearance, kindness, goodness, faithfulness, gentleness and self-control. Against such things there is no law."

"*Love? Love? LOVE? Are you there? Where did you go? Can you respond so that I can feel your presence? Love is a small word with huge meaning! Everyone claims to love but don't truly know what love means,*" Brittany thought. She sat back and observed the huge word as she thought about so many couples surrounding her. She watched the four-letter word get thrown around so easily and uncaringly. However, she strongly feels it's a powerful word just like the word *hate*. She wanted to do her best to avoid falling in love until the evening of Sunday, September 13th. On that day, she expressed, "I'm ready to take the high road with you and take a chance at a life together." "*Why not? We've been friends and flirting since preschool,*" she thought.

Brittany's first experience when seeing love or lust from a boy was a huge disaster. She decided to give an immature, insecure, disgusting, arrogant, scumbag of a guy named Samuel aka Sammy a chance. Coming from a loving family who tried their best to bring her up properly, Brittany felt every bit of out of place being in some situations that she endured with Sammy. Though it may seem small, for no reason, she endured being called things other than what her mother named her at birth.

She quickly realized she didn't like what love was starting to look like from that angle. It was far from what she had seen from the generations before her. It looked nothing like the love stories she had witnessed from her role models. She thought maybe it was her fault and that she pushed him to talk to her that way. When Brittany decided that the love she had wasn't right, she chose to take a break and be a loner. It wasn't a big deal because she was young and knew that she had a life ahead. She knew she would see affectionate love again. She was hoping that the next shot at it would be different. Much different!

Brittany could never deny the experience she had with Sammy from the way he talked to her, tried to manipulate her, talked to women around her, control her, accused her, and more. The pain she felt was much worse during the experience than she could ever explain. The guilt from his actions made him insecure with his position in her life. One day, Sammy picked Brittany up and took her to get some ice cream. They smiled and bonded as they enjoyed the evening. Sammy decided to take her to the mall as well, so she could pick out her outfit for the night's plans. While they were walking through the mall and browsing the stores, Sammy instantly snapped. Brittany was embarrassed.

"What is your problem, Samuel?" she asked.

He said, "You're always in some man's face."

She didn't know what he was talking about, so she gave him a confused look.

He said, "Yeah, play stupid. I saw how you looked at him. How do you think I feel? From man to man, if he assumes my girl is in his face, I look weak."

"Did he say this to you?"

She paused for a second waiting for a response.

"No?" she asked.

He stayed silent, so she responded, "Okay, soooo this is your assumption. We walked past several women, and I made eye contact with them without a death stare. A guy who's not even my type walks pass, and you flip?"

If Brittany even looked at a man, Sammy would instantly start an argument. In his mind, a quick look meant they were going to be on a date tomorrow and in the bed the next day. At the beginning of the relationship, Brittany had no idea that he lived with major insecurities. After a short while, it was quickly exposed. Why was she attracted to this "bad boy, rude boy" knowing she prayed for the total opposite? He sold drugs heavily and owned weapons. He was far out of her interest, but something about her flesh had her attached to him. *"What do you do when you are dealing with someone who doesn't share the same beliefs?"* she thought after getting deeper involved.

Sammy and Brittany did not share the same spiritual beliefs. No matter how much she tried to agree with Sammy, their views were always so different. She was young and didn't quite understand why he acted in such a manner. Brittany always tried to find the good in people. However, she wasn't real with herself by facing the truth. The more she began to pray the more she saw him stray. One night when Sammy's cousin, Lafayette, was at the house, he asked Brittany if she had any friends.

She said, "Maybe."

Although she had plenty of friendships, she would not set her friends up if he was no good. Brittany was very protective over her loved ones. After she observed Lafayette's personality, a light bulb went off on which friend she thought could be a great match for him. Brittany called her homegirl, Melissa, on video chat and allowed Lafayette to ask her out himself. She felt he needed to captivate Melissa's mind if he wanted her. If he couldn't do so, then no time needed to be wasted.

Later that evening, they went to pick Melissa up and decided to go on a double date to the movies. The movie was amazing. Both couples left out with smiles, jokes, and laughter. Melissa and Lafayette said the joke from the movie, and Brittany laughed. In a matter of seconds, Sammy had become so withdrawn. He was still talking amongst them, but his attitude had changed. When they got in the car, they all noticed that something was wrong.

They kept asking, "What's wrong?"

In a soft tone, he kept saying, "Nothing."

As much as Brittany wanted just to leave him alone, it became awkward. She almost felt like the third wheel entertaining Lafayette and Melissa. So, she rode in silence the whole ride. When they pulled up to the house and entered the sitting area, Sammy dismissed himself.

While still in the sitting area, Lafayette and Melissa started kissing. Although it was cute and all, Brittany was still stuck on the fact Sammy left the room. She couldn't believe how bipolar he was. He would ruin every nice event or a good outing.

As Brittany grabbed her phone to leave, Melissa said, "Where are you going, Poo?"

Brittany responded, "Did it seem like something went wrong, or am I tripping?"

They replied, "We saw the change but don't understand what happened."

It was a mystery to all. Lafayette and Melissa didn't care though. They had each other. As Brittany proceeded down the hall, she heard Sammy in the other room on the phone. The call was on speaker. Brittany could hear another girl talking negatively about her. *"How is he allowing anyone to bad mouth me?"* she thought.

As she listened to the call, she heard him say, "She thinks she can keep disrespecting me, so let her sit in there."

Brittany interrupted their conversation. "Excuse me?"

"Man, what?" he said.

The girl on the phone said, "You want to call me back?"

He replied, "Yes."

Brittany said, "No if you can say it behind my back, share it with me."

Sammy asked her to chill and hung the phone up.

Before he could say anything else, Brittany responded, "First, you could easily tell me to go home. I would not invade your privacy. Second, don't ever talk about me behind my back when I'm available to be addressed. Third, don't ever think this is cool to talk to other females while dating me, and don't downplay me to any of them. Lastly, if I'm such a problem, I'll solve this by ending it."

As Brittany prepared to leave the room, Sammy grabbed her arm in full aggression.

"Watch how you talk to me like a man! Learn your place."

She said, "My place is now your EX-girlfriend."

Sammy told her she was a promiscuous woman and would forever be one. He told her he knew her kind. He then laughed in a wicked way that wasn't genuine.

"I saw you look at my cousin."

Brittany chuckled and said, "Wait, so because I looked at someone who's talking to me, this is where all this started?"

He grabbed her up and said, "You are so disrespectful. That's why I got female friends, to answer your question because I know the type of girl you are."

Brittany's laugh became anger and hurt. How could he insult her character? She is so pure and easygoing, yet his mind has created a corrupt and negative image of her. Brittany's mind was rambling. She was extremely confused. They were having a good time, and something so innocent became so intense.

"When any man speaks, I should just look away?" she asked.

She couldn't believe what she was hearing. Not to mention, she was still a virgin who had fallen into deep lust over him but got called every bad name in the book. He got even more upset with her question in addition to hearing the new couple exchanging laughter, conversation, and kissing noises.

He asked, "Why haven't you had sex with me yet? You are acting childish, and that shows you don't love me!" Brittany had never seen such nitpicking and manipulation in her life until then. He did well in the beginning and didn't show his truth until her feelings were deeply involved.

As Brittany was getting ready to respond, he cut her off. His phone rang, so he answered and engaged back into the conversation with a girl named Nadia. It made Brittany extremely angry, but she knew that arguing wouldn't solve the issue. She wasn't just mad at him. She was mad that another woman could be this foul to listen to him disrespect her and think he would be different to her. Any normal girl didn't think on a woman-to-woman basis. They would be ready to fight and keep pushing, but not Brittany. She had the gift to minimize someone's character most politely. The person would only be able to take heed and respect what was said, even if they didn't show it at that time.

With tears in her eyes, she told him, "its best you carry on because this shows me that you made a choice. Take care!"

Unfortunately, that was the moment Brittany lost her mind and became dumbfounded. She allowed him to speak more lies and sweet talk. When he saw her tears, he knew he hit a nerve and stroked her vulnerability, so he apologized. Brittany started to hear more and more apologies as their relationship continued. The relationship had good moments, but when the bad surfaced, it was really bad. Brittany grew a tough skin and started to attack back with words. He eventually began to disrespect the relationship blatantly.

The cheating got worse as he exchanged disgraceful messages with many different women. He even arranged dates behind her back. When Brittany wasn't around, he had countless inappropriate private conversations with other women. He began to answer Nadia's call in Brittany's presence. One day, Brittany was talking to him without knowing who was on the phone.

Referring to Brittany, he told the female on the phone, "My Sis is talking."

However, he said it in a way that made Brittany think he was telling her that his sister was on the phone. Imagine how Brittany felt when she realized that wasn't his sister. Coincidentally, his sister entered the house at that moment. The player was boldly showing her that she meant nothing to him. That hurt Britt deeply because she couldn't quite understand why she was going through this. She had done nothing to reap such behavior. Brittany still was foolish enough to answer when he called, so it wasn't all his fault. One day, she no longer stood as the fool. Sammy called to inform her that he and Nadia had sex a few times and that she was pregnant. She processed that information for a moment.

Then, she smiled and said, "Well, congratulations."

A voice spoke chimed in, "Ay, bro, I think she thinks you're playing."

This clown called Brittany with Lafayette on the phone.

"Sweetheart, it's not that I don't believe him. I believe there's more to this. Truthfully, I don't need to know what that is because it's none of my business. God showed me this for some time now. I knew he wasn't the one for me, but I allowed his sweet talks to manipulate me into staying," she laughed. "This time, he can't! This is the best bad news I've had in a while, and now my blinders are off to see that I deserve much more. So, I'm smiling because God saved me from someone who was no good. So, I say again, Sammy, Congratulations!"

Brittany left them wondering how more bad news was a blessing. Before Brittany could hang up, Sammy asked Lafayette to hang up. Britt thought that was hilarious because he shouldn't have ever been on the phone.

He said, "Boo."

She stayed quiet.

He said, "Baby."

She remained quiet.

He asked, "Are you okay? Are you crying?"

She responded, "Yes, I'm okay, and hell no I'm not crying."

"Well, why are you so quiet?"

She said, "Ohhh, that's only because I thought you were speaking to Nadia. I apologize. My name is Brittany, and that's what I would like you to address me as."

He replied, "Brittany, I apologize."

However, she didn't need an apology. She didn't need anything but to hang that phone up and release that toxic relationship. Although that's her truth, she still allowed him to speak. She found out in small talk that he had abused Nadia, and she was threatening to tell Brittany about the baby, so he confessed.

Brittany had warned Nadia before. Sammy had never hit Brittany, but he was aggressive in how he handled her sometimes. She dodged that one! When he first broke the news, she was hurt because his actions were so foul. Brittany wondered how he'd get to be happy and start this family and leave her broken. She thought it was the end of her love life. He damaged her, broke her trust, and made her feel a little insecure because of the other women. Then, she realized she wasn't the problem. All along, it was him who wasn't so happy after all.

As much as Brittany wanted to cheer, she humbly said, "Thanks, Sammy, for being honest. I don't hate you! I thank you because you taught me something precious."

He asked, "And, what's that?"

She further explained, "Every relationship is a step stool to the next level of dating for me to find my husband. It's only increasing my character and building strength. So, Sam-"

He cut her off in the middle of her speaking and said, "Can you be the godmother?"

Brittany paused, and then responded with a slick laugh, "Are you serious?"

He said, "Yeah. I feel you are a good person and I would never want to lose you."

She responded, "My question wasn't in awe. It was to inform you that you sound foolish. I would never accept that offer."

He said, "Well, can we remain friends?"

She said, "No, but I'll forever wish you well."

When she told him she had to end the call, his voice started to change as if tears filled his eyes. Brittany was over it at that point. She couldn't care less as she hung up. She had to take some time to herself. During that time, she chose to learn the true meaning of love and not to make that mistake again. She often meditated on 1 Corinthians 13:4-8.

Love Is

Love is patient.
Love is kind.
Love does not envy or boast.
Love is not self- seeking or easily angered.
Love keeps no record of wrongs.
Love does not delight in evil but rejoices with the truth.
Love always to protect, trust, hopes and perseveres.

Reminder:

Although Brittany took time to learn what love is after a bad relationship, it's still fearful when brokenness is in place. Perfect love that comes from God casts out all fear. Fear and faith are opposite like love and hate. They don't go hand and hand. Some relationships can cause heartbreak, confusion, and more but try to stay peaceful! No matter how much pain you endured from the heartbreak, it's our job to forgive as Christ forgave us. Truthfully, to get past the pain, the Bible instructs us not to self-seek. That simply means your flesh and mind can steer you wrong at times, so you must always seek God's face and put Him first.

You must trust in God. Believe that everything you face in life will work together for your good. I can admit that this is way easier said than done! I can guarantee you that it can be done though. No matter what I had learned during my seasons of heartbreaks, my ignorance of the studies of the word was at an all-time high.

What God has for you is for you. You will know if someone is the right one for you because God will reveal it. Remember to watch the fruit of their labor! From a religious view, it's best that you stop pursuing a person if they are not willing to give their life to Christ and study His word. This should be confirmed before marriage. If you are religious and considering marrying someone who does not believe in Christ, you two are "unequally yoked." 2 Corinthians 6:14 says, "Do not be yoked together with unbelievers. What do righteousness and wickedness have in common or what fellowship can light share with darkness?" This is not conflicting with the fact that you should love your neighbor. It's stating that when you are engaged deeper with a non-believer exchanging sexual desires and connecting your souls, you allow things to corrupt in your spirit that God prefers you to avoid. This is a command that's designed to protect you. Always watch the fruit of the Spirit.

Question:

What qualities are you looking for in your spouse?

_____
_____
_____
_____
_____
_____
_____
_____
_____
_____
_____
_____
_____
_____
_____
_____
_____
_____
_____

Sow the seed by writing a short prayer and allowing God to manifest.

_____
_____
_____
_____
_____
_____

Chapter 8

How Did He Rape My Confidence?

Proverbs 3:26

*"For the LORD will be at your side and will keep your
foot from being snared."*

The sun began to set on Wednesday at 5:00 p.m.
Michelle was cutting thick chicken breasts into small
chunks for Kevin's favorite dish. He loved chicken alfredo
with a biscuit and a glass of ice-cold fruit punch on the
side. He says the fruit punch gives him the appearance that
he's drinking wine, except he hates wine. He prefers water,
but he would make an exception for this meal. Michelle
believed home is more than a physical building. Home is
where the heart is! She would always have the clothes
washed and folded, house clean, uniforms ironed, bed
made, and dinner ready for Kevin.

As Michelle drove to work each day, she passed a
small white and green house. She never really noticed the
house until the grass grew as tall as the windows. That
house had been abandoned for so long, so Michelle went
home to check the market of the home. Based on the
picture, it wasn't the same image she saw in person. The air
conditioning unit was missing, and some of the beautiful
details of the home were not visible.

From the looks of that house, it no longer felt like a
home. It almost looked like a crowded cobweb home on
scary movies. However, that didn't mean it couldn't be
touched up, cleaned, and redecorated! It simply symbolized

that when things become abandoned too long, they become broken down, molded, and even burglarized. Michelle's interest in the house made Kevin curious, so he decided to see the house for himself. He was disappointed when he saw the outside of the home. He wondered what she could admire about this rundown property.

One evening, Michelle ran herself a bath that was so hot that it could burn her skin. Her goal was to detox and wind down. She'd had a long work week, so the heat relaxed her aching muscles. As the water filled the tub, she picked out a cute set of pajamas to wear in hopes to impress her boo. As she looked in the right top drawer where she kept a few of her toys, she chuckled. She was reminded of the fun nights they'd shared with them. She quickly closed the drawer and ran to turn the water off.

Buzz… Buzz… Buzz…

Michelle heard the vibration sound of a phone in the bedroom. However, her phone was in the bathroom. As she followed the sound, she realized Kevin left his work phone. The phone rang again. Someone was calling from the main office line, so Michelle answered with the company motto as if she was a coworker.

"Thanks for calling CID agents where we can fix it. Michelle, speaking how may I help you?" The voice on the other end happened to be Kevin calling to make sure he had not lost his phone.

He laughed and said, "Don't be saying my motto, and then adding your name."

"Well, how did I do?"

"You did great bae. No one will ever notice that squeaky voice."

She laughed and said, "Love you, Stink."

Before ending the conversation, he responded, "I love you, too, bae. I'll be there to get the phone, but I'm going to the gym this evening. So, don't wait up."

Michelle entered the tub with anger all over her face. She was expecting a nice night, but he once again made plans to be out. It's been said three times' a charm, but in her case, three days in a row he chose to be in the gym with no regards to her feelings. This was not so charming. As she twirled the only curly piece hanging from her bun, she compared the abandoned house to her relationship. The emotions start to break down like the walls of the home. The communication becomes toxic like the mold forming around the wet areas. The devil steals, kills, and destroys everything left just like the people who took that air conditioner and a few other belongings. She was so upset internally, but she tried to fix it when she heard the front door close.

Kevin came upstairs, grabbed his phone, and then stuck his head in the bathroom to kiss Michelle. Although she loved his 6'4" height kneeling to kiss her with those thick juicy lips, she had to fight back the tears. She was tired of laying in their fully furnished house alone. When he wasn't there, it felt like an empty home. Michelle's heart was in a place she thought was home. To her, home was a place that protects you from the rain, covers all your needs, keeps the heart and body warm, and more! She had been keeping busy feeding into their home so much, thinking it was special! However, she failed to realize the home had been abandoned and betrayed for some time.

Once Kevin left, she grabbed her phone and went directly to the notes. She started writing what she had noticed:

"I went home countless days and night to an empty home. I was cooking dinner for two but eating alone. I've been packing dinner for tomorrow for a lunch that never got eaten. He'd lie and say, 'Oh, and my food was good!' Meanwhile, he just was occupied and always on the go. He did it so much that he paid no attention to anything I did. I□ tried to jazz it up to be sexy. I would shower and slip into lingerie before he stepped foot home. Now that I think about it, nothing is keeping him from making small pitstop home and actually being here bonding with me!"

Michelle sat there a little longer, and the tears started flowing. Her intuition informed her that she had something to worry about, but she never caught it red-handed. So, she could only assume that he was just busy. As she sat thinking about her relationship, her phone started ringing. It was her homegirl, Angie. She was the best person for Michelle to talk to, but her approach to everything is so hood and straightforward that Michelle just wasn't ready for that type of conversation. As soon as the phone stopped ringing, Angie number came up again. So, Michelle answered in a low tone as if she couldn't talk right then. There were no hard feelings towards Angie. The situation was just getting the best of her.

Angie said, "Monkey, I'm at the door!"

"Girl, I was in the bathtub. Give me a moment," Michelle said.

"No rush. I'll sit in the car for a little while."

Michelle relaxed a little longer and kept writing. As she stood up and dried off, she put her robe on to let Angie in.

Angie joked, "Monkey, girl, you still dirty."

Usually, Michelle would joke back, but her heart was aching from the thought of another night of expected loneliness. Angie noticed her humor wasn't right.

"What's wrong with you?" Angie said.

"I was relaxing."

They went upstairs, and Michelle began applying lotion to her body. Angie cut to the chase.

"Are you and Kevin still together?"

"Duh, girl. He just left our house. If those vows stand, good or bad, we're together," Michelle said with a slight chuckle.

From the look of Angie's face, this wasn't a joking matter.

Michelle said, "Why you ask?"

Angie replied, "Well, you been hanging with us more. You know when he's around, you kick us to the curb."

Angie was fishing to see if Monkey was covering up the truth.

"Girl, he is so busy. It's only right that I keep myself busy, too," Michelle said.

"Monkey, I don't know what he's telling you, but his actions are not adding up," Angie said.

In Michelle mind, she replied, *"Girl that's what's I'm saying,"* but her heart was trembling trying to figure out why her friend was saying that.

Michelle blurted out, "I don't know what's going on. I addressed some things about a female interfering in our relationship when we were boyfriend and girlfriend. We were not married. Man, when we got married, I assumed he was ready. He lined it all up for us to be under one covenant as he felt God would love. The way he talked about God, the way he talked about couple's things, the visions he shared, and the attempt to change! I☐ was so deeply in love that I☐ fell for it!"

Angie said, "Well, maybe he did change. I'm just hoping he finds more time for you."

Michelle kept venting. "It meant everything to me to finally get that new guy! Please do not tell me this fat lip, tall, slinky man messed up!"

Her friend said, "This is not a funny moment, but the things you love most about him, you just used to talk about him."

Michelle laughed and said, "I always do that once I'm mad. Everyone knows I'm not serious about what I call him. I'm just mad."

Angie said, "Oh, I know. But, why are you so mad?"

"Yeah, I just jumped the gun because I feel something. I just don't know what," Michelle said.

Angie responded, "I've been seeing him and this girl together. I think she's a coworker because the clothes she had on looks like the uniforms he wears."

Michelle said, "Wait, what?"

She said, "Yes. I even have a video," she said as she looked through her purse to find her phone. "I'm going to show you."

As Michelle's heart raced with the fear of the unknown, she said, "Yes, because my man will deny it. He will have me to cut you off if this isn't proven." Angie responded, "He will never be able to have you cut me off. If he cares about your happiness, he would understand I'm a real friend. I came all the way over here to tell you, so you don't have to feel alone after seeing it."

"How in the world did I not allow myself to believe my intuition? Michelle thought to herself. As she looked at

the video, her mind started racing. A brown skin girl was leaning back on Kevin as if they were a couple. She thought, *"If I approach it this way, he may respond that way. If I hold back, then I may react in a bad way."* She was trying to see if she should hold out with approaching him to see if he's going to the gym tonight. She couldn't figure out the best way to address the situation. The video was not too extreme, but the way his arm was around her was obvious that they had something more than "pass me this" at work!

"Forget it. I can't hold back; I'm about to call him."

Angie said, "Wait, what will you say?"

She said, "I can't tell you because when I get on the phone, I may not say any of it. It all depends on his responses."

As the phone rung, Michelle practiced how she is going to respond. Kevin didn't answer. Michelle sent a text "EMERGENCY!"

Angie said, "Take a deep breath so you can get everything out and not forget any of your questions from being super mad."

Michelle agreed and took a sip of water. Kevin called quickly. He couldn't get the full greeting out.

"Bae is everyth-"

"Stink, do you love me?"

He said, "Yes, now what's so important right now?"

Michelle began to boil. "So important? Me asking you about love isn't important?"

He said, "Are you okay? What's wrong?"

"Do you love me, Kevin? Strongly?"

He replied, "I said yes, Michelle. You know I am at work. What is wrong?"

She paused and took a deep breath.

"Here it is. Do you talk to one of your coworkers? I hope not because the last time you talked to one, you know how that turned out. I forgave you once. I can't do this again."

She didn't give him a moment to speak.

He stopped her and said, "Look, man, I don't have time for this," and hung up.

That hurt Michelle's heart. As she fought back the tears, she said, "What does he mean he doesn't have time? I come first, and I need reassurance."

She called again, but he sent her to voicemail.

Michelle said, "Well, since he is ignoring me. Let's see you ignore your family and friends, too."

She sent the video in a group to everyone on both sides and included him in it.

Angie said, "You shouldn't have done that. Keep your business to yourself."

"Maybe you're right, but I'm furious and tired of him disrespecting me when times are hard. I'm tired of being ignored, tired of being pushed to the back, and tired of seeing him give me dry greetings, but he's in this video looking happy. I'm tired of feeling he's lying to me. I'M TIRED," she screamed, and tears started flowing.

While Angie was hugging Michelle as she vented about her problems, the responses from the family came back quickly.

What is this? Who is this? The messages grabbed his attention so fast.

Kevin called her back and said, "Baby, why did you send that to everyone?"

"You won't answer to me, so answer to them when they are wondering where I've gone."

"Gone?"

"Yes, I will not sit here and be humiliated like this."

He said, "Baby, it's not what it looks like!"

When she asked questions before, he didn't have time. He knew what he had done, but because he thought she didn't know, it was okay to ignore her. Only ten minutes after he realized she had evidence, he couldn't help but respond to her. After seeing his family responding and calling him, he suddenly had all the time to talk about this.

She responded, "Look you're at work, so just like you don't have time, I don't have time for this."

He said, "Why are you doing this?"

She simply said, "The same way you responded earlier, keep that same energy."

At first, he didn't care about her feelings towards the situation. She was fully aware of that. Now, he didn't like that his image was getting ready to take a turn. He was a good guy gone bad in the eyes of those he inspires. She protected his image for so long, but she didn't care anymore. She knew her home was empty, but she thought he was willing to change. She thought his actions were only temporary. She figured maybe he just needed space to clear his mind. Still, she wondered where he was going all those gym nights. She used to tell herself she was going to stay up to catch him. However, before he could come home for her to see anything suspicious, she would fall asleep. She knew that one day it would reveal itself, so she stopped searching.

Kevin wanted to fix the situation for the public eye. He wanted to talk to her mom to make it better, talk to her friends to explain further, and only God knows what he expressed to his own family to clear his name. What no one knew, including Michelle, was that Kevin had been involved with other women during the nine years they had been together. Not all the involvements were sexual, but they shouldn't have been interacting, conversing, or anything else. When people would tell Michelle things, Kevin would lie and say those people were jealous of the marriage. Because no one gave proof, she fell victim to believing him. She protected his image even though she knew she didn't see his ring the countless nights he said he was at the gym.

She saw a change in the way he talked and handled things, but she couldn't react the way she wanted to just yet. She had to have evidence because he would make her believe people didn't want to see them happy. There were some who didn't want to see them happy, but she couldn't distinguish the two. This time, she had proof that he was way too friendly with females behind her back.

As she soaked in pain, she said emotionally, "It's time for a break," and hung up.

It wasn't that she wanted the break, but he gave her no other choice! His actions let her know that he wasn't ready to commit no matter how much she did. Kevin hated those words. He never saw himself getting caught cheating. He was so smooth, and she was too trusting.

He called her back and said, "I apologize. It's not what it looks like."

Michelle responded, "I can't wait until I☐ have a disease to walk away, Kevin."

He said, "I didn't have sexual relations."

Truthfully, she didn't know if he did. She had no proof of it, so she could only react to what she saw in the video. He said he didn't interact with ladies, but that turned out to be a lie. Kevin's family started calling and texting saying they didn't understand the video. As she explained what took place, they said they couldn't understand what got into him. They came up with plots and plans to make him feel the pain, but it wasn't worth it.

Michelle said, "I don't have time for the games. I'm done. I'm leaving."

Those words created judgment.

"No, I didn't say leave. Leaving isn't the answer to your vows. You need to stay. You haven't even fought long. You haven't been married long. I've done worse to my spouse, or my spouse has done worse to me," her family said.

Michelle grew angry at them and their responses. She felt they were minimizing her pain. She had prayed and cried many nights. Sadness filled her days. She and Kevin slept in separate bedrooms as she could no longer look at him. She couldn't believe that there were so many people with something to say about her making a smart decision for her marriage. When she got up and did what she felt was best, they weren't there to hold him accountable. No one had to live with that pain except Michelle.

Michelle got up for church the following Sunday morning with hopes to get a message in the word. Nevertheless, a negative spirit took over her mind. She laid in bed outraged at the pain that took over, the humiliation it caused, and the judgment as if she was wrong. She couldn't stomach the pain. So, she went to the bathroom and grabbed a bottle of pills that read: *Adults take up to 2 tablets every 6 hours*. She decided to take more. She thought about how family, friends, and even the church had asked her to stay in her broken marriage. No one had answers as to why she should accept his actions. They would only say, "The bible says so."

No one knew she tried to harm herself. No one knew the depths of her failing heart. As her heart trembled with fear, she thought about God revealed to her after prayers. Even when she kept telling the family that she was hearing God's voice, they still told her to be careful because it might be the enemy. None of them considered the possibility that God could be telling them to separate. *"So, the enemy is more powerful than God, in your opinion?"* she thought. They were against anything that resembled walking away.

Michelle told the family, "I'm confused. Adultery is a sin - a gateway out, and you all are trying to convince me to stay. Who's to say God doesn't want more for me?"

They would respond, "You take everything as a sign and perceive wrong messages sometimes. The Bible says Gods hate divorce."

Their point had Michelle contemplating staying. However, she refused to allow the cheating. She became furious at the thought.

"You are quoting scriptures at me when He doesn't want His child dealing with abuse. It may not be physical, but the mental and emotional abuse is just as bad. Yes, it can be worked on, but it's not just one woman. There have been multiple women!" she said with frustration and walked away.

No matter if she went back, the trust would have never been the same because he constantly entertained other women. So, what, he wrote the girl a long message on choosing his wife. However, based on the other women, it wouldn't be hard for him to get another woman. Therefore, that long message didn't even matter. At this point, Michelle started being hard on herself. She began comparing herself to the other women. She wondered why they were better than she was what made them worth losing everything. Michelle was destroyed and damaged. Kevin ruined her confidence and self-esteem. She couldn't even look herself in the mirror.

Michelle decided to visit another church. The pastor read from 1 Peter:4, "The enemy doesn't start by hitting your physical being, finances or marriage. He starts first with your mind." That pastor spoke to Michelle separately, "He has to heat some things to work on you. Take time to be in this singleness so that you and God can have one-on-one time. Anything you are attached to and longing for, let it go. God must deal with it. Any relationship outside of God's relationship is seasonal. Even if you say 'til death do us part, it's not eternal like God's relationship afterlife. The enemy came in like a flood, but God is getting ready to pour out His blessings upon you."

Michelle walked out feeling new. She ignored the people who told her it was not right to leave. She heard what she needed to hear. The pastor never said get a divorce. He simply said for her to let it go because God must deal with it. Therefore, separation was not a crime in her marriage. It had gotten too extreme. It was a fight she couldn't win on her own. She had to let it go and put her husband and the situation in God's hand. That's what she did. In the meantime, it wasn't about what God would do to him. Her concern was what she needed to gain from God in that singleness stage.

Reminder:

God sends confirmation in threes. When you are holding on to someone when God said let go, you will allow the bad to overpower if you are not obedient to His voice. If you are not married, do not hold on because of years or kids. Holding on to things because of history can prevent you from connecting to your destiny. He is protecting you from something the eyes have yet seen, so you would have to try to push through with trust. However, trust as small as a mustard seed is all you need. Having more trust in God is always good, but a teeny amount is all it takes.

When God speaks, do not test the waters by moving too fast to see what He has in store for you. Rushing the process can lead you to some major hardship. When God taps into your attachments, He starts dealing with your internal issues. He wants His babies to abide in amazing situations. We can't always blame God because of our disobedience. We are often afraid of the unknown and anxious to see the greater He has for us because we are holding on to what we are complacent within our lives. If you don't move when He says so, God will allow pain to manifest in your life so that you have no choice but to move forward.

I do not encourage divorce. God hates it. However, don't get married if you are not seriously ready. Understand that you can't leave because he irritates you, finances are low, and other issues have arisen. God speaks on adultery as well. However, God is bigger and can change people. Just don't be a fool. As sad as it is and as hard as it may be, it will be for your greater good, in the end, to seek God first before taking any steps into commitments. Pay attention to the signs and watch the fruit! I wouldn't want time wasted and another unsolicited heartbreak to occur.

Question:

Write about a time when you had to decide against what people said and/or what you felt. Which did you choose, and was your choice beneficial in the end?

Chapter 9

How to Get Past the Pain
Once It's Embedded in Your Heart

Joshua 1:9

*"Have I not commanded you? Be strong and courageous.
Do not be afraid; do not be discouraged, for the LORD
your God will be with you wherever you go."*

Sherice jumped up quickly. She was sweating and looking around the room to notice that she was only dreaming. She took a deep breath and sat in silence trying to figure out what her dream could've meant. It was so detailed. However, as soon as she woke up, she instantly began to forget the dream. All she could remember was that it was about her boyfriend, Bernard.

Sherice was a shy but sassy, loving but stubborn, forgiving but angry young woman. She was never really one that was afraid to give her all. However, after being hurt, betrayed and damaged, you sort of hold back! But she couldn't understand why she was running from the guy that could be "the one." Why was she punishing the new guy for the old guy's actions? Why couldn't he get a fair shot? Why was Sherice letting past pain keep her from staying interested?

She asked herself, "What could I possibly imagine going wrong in a place I felt was designed just for me?"

She had her girls who held her down, a family who always supported, and most of all, the church who kept her in prayer! Her spirit was happy, peaceful and full of joy.

Furthermore, she had a smile that is vibrant and contagious. If you got to know her, you would say she couldn't be happier! Some individuals would say they adored Sherice's happiness! They would even wish they had the blessings upon her. As she went through life day to day, she experienced being goals for some and the W.C.W. (Women Crush Wednesday on social media) for others just for being herself! These individuals admired all her strength and wished to obtain it.

But...

Sherice had grown weary and tired from working long hours. She worked so much on both jobs that she had no free time to enjoy a little bit of life. So, she took a pay cut to be happy and spend time with family and friends. At the time of making the decision, it was very stressful. She had to weigh her pros and cons to make sure everything was aligned. People said she was lucky to have all that she did, but what they failed at realizing was that she put in work to have it. She sacrificed a lot. She knew what she wanted. Working overnight wasn't her choice anymore.

As she rushed up from her dream and looked at the clock, she thought, *"It's only 8:24 p.m.?"* Sitting within those four walls for some time just scrolling through her phone was causing time to move fast but so slow. Sherice couldn't believe he had yet to call. He hadn't even bothered to apologize for hanging up a few hours ago. She had driven home from work in good spirits and called her man Bernard. He talked to her briefly, but she thought he was acting weird. He sounded as if we were available to talk for a moment. Seconds later, he sounded like something or someone surrounded him. Sherice's intuition screamed.

Although she thought something was off, she didn't let it get the best of her and send any bad vibes. As she noticed him addressing her with an attitude as if he wanted her to be mad so that they wouldn't talk the rest of the day, she felt that was another red flag. She heard a door close in his background, and he instantly hung up. Sherice wasn't the type to press and blow up any man's phone, but she did call back to make sure his phone didn't die. The phone rung normally. However, he didn't answer, nor did he bother calling back. She knew something strange was going on, but she wasn't sure if she was ready to know the unknown.

Truthfully, no one knew she felt so weak behind the scenes. When people said they wanted a life like hers, Sherice wanted to tell them to be careful what you wish, ask, or pray for because you just might get it. Images are always angled, filtered, and adjusted to capture the beauty. However, you are not able to see the bloopers like the tears a baby cried before capturing their first photo. As she started to be home more, she realized that her boyfriend wasn't living how she thought he was. He had too much time on his hands to continuously make poor choices. So why did she stick around? What made him so special when so many other guys wanted her?

Sherice walked with a confident attitude. She was a young lady who wanted more for herself, but she didn't quite understand why she couldn't receive it. Her heart was pure as she gave her full compassion to Bernard. Unfortunately, she kept attracting herself to the wrong man. In this case, Sherice had an extremely toxic long-term relationship with Bernard. He bought her love, and his actions showed it. He just wasn't ready to settle down, but he didn't want to let go either.

Sadly, Sherice stayed with him and endured all that came with the relationship. As much as she knew it wasn't right, her heart was attached. She dealt with fighting over her man, fighting her man, and fighting herself with decision making. He always promised he would get better. He claimed he would commit this time. He promised again! He said he would not hurt her this time. He promised he would never leave her alone. He said they would grow through it, but Sherice felt the relationship was far from growth. In fact, she felt he was only destroying the little she had to offer.

He was starting to take advantage of her. She saw it, but her heart wouldn't allow her to move how she wish she could. She figured people go through the ugly stages in a relationship without realizing they are getting exactly what they wanted. Then, they wonder "God, why me?" Although people idolized her, she was not obligated to share every detail in her life. She learned that people are not always on her side, so it was best to keep information to herself.

There had been days when Sherice would have the biggest smile and received the best compliment while holding back tears. People would think the tears were for one thing when deep inside she didn't know how much longer she could continue with the act of being strong. It even got to the point that friends and family couldn't tell she had been suffering deep within.

Sherice's pain came from putting her heart into the hands of a man. Her mind told her to walk away and keep dating, but her heart was so deeply attached! The cheating, lies, and games began to be so overwhelming. She was tired of hearing, "I'm sorry." Even that was like pulling teeth. Sometimes she sought answers so that her mind wouldn't assume the worst. She would ask for an apology knowing he wasn't sorry or was too prideful to apologize. She was left to cry herself to sleep yet again.

Sherice listened as people praised Bernard's name. They talked about how great of a guy he was. However, at night she had to wonder what club he may have been at and if there was another girl. Soon after her anxiety cooled down and her tears dried, she pumped herself up to leave him. She knew the "Baby, it was a mistake" line was coming. Nevertheless, she fell for it.

The worse the cheating became, the more she started to hate the women. Truthfully, she knew they weren't at fault; they only did what he allowed. Sherice started to hate Bernard. Her heart was there, but her flesh couldn't stand him. She started not to want to have sex with him or do anything for him because she felt stupid the more, she did for him. It was like she was rewarding bad behavior. Still, Sherice battled the thought of her relationship in shambles.

As they quickly forgot the pain Bernard caused in private, they allowed make-up sex to save the day for their madness. Sherice admired his physical appearance. The sad part was that the same appearance she admired was the appearance the world also admired. Bernard was so big on himself that he didn't realize that he was selfish towards her feelings. He hadn't recognized the new things she liked, the changes in friendships, or the fact that she even changed her hair.

So many women were so attached to Bernard's looks that they didn't even care that he had the main woman at home. It didn't matter if they cared or not. All that mattered was if he cared enough to reject the women.

Still, the more Sherice told herself to leave him, the more her treasure box got excited for him. The more she smiled, the more her heart cried. The more she prayed, the more things started to separate. Their broken relationship hurt her heart deeply. She couldn't see why God didn't want their relationship to be.

As Sherice started to fall into temptation, God started small by allowing him to upset her with white lies. It was just enough to make her say, "Look, I'm done you constantly lying," but not enough to feel it was tragic enough to leave. Then, she realized the lies became stronger. Women were being hidden, conversations were being muted, lies were growing bigger, and he was having sex with the other women. With tears in her eyes, she wondered why Bernard would give her false hope. He was constantly making promises he could barely remember. They were covered deeply in all his lies as he made her believe she meant everything to him.

Sherice wished for him to become a better mate. Eventually, she pulled back because the pain became unbearable. He cut her in a way that no other man could because he was her best friend before anything else. Before they even pursued the relationship, she had already feared crossing that path. However, her heartbeat big for him, so she felt he was worth the try.

As days and weeks went by, his tone became thorough, his attitude became strong, his moods were negative, and his gentle touch became aggressive. She knew the relationship was shifting, yet it was hard for her to see it. Better yet, it was hard to accept it. She was everything you could want in a female but dealing with Bernard made her feel the emptiest. She wondered how he could claim to love her, but as soon as he got upset, her name went from Ricey, baby, or beautiful to hoe and slut.

He once claimed his love for her was strong and that she meant the world to him. That only came after she restricted him from sex. She wondered why the lack of sex made him change as if that's all she had to offer. She decided to stop having sex with Bernard because she realized he didn't respect her body. When he came around, he couldn't stop himself from touching her. Sherice finally realized he wasn't focused on her heart and mind as he had been in the past. He would only be thinking about the next time she would open her legs for him again. She felt low as she looked him in his eyes and noticed she wasn't worth the wait for him. She knew in her gut that he had moved on and was just holding on to a consistent sexual lifestyle.

As much as she hated him for lying, stealing her heart, and cheating on her, her heart wouldn't allow her to let go. She told herself, "Don't you dare write another message," but her fingers wouldn't stop typing. She said she would never answer another call, but as soon as he called, she answered on the first ring. The pain she felt grew so big, and he had become so careless to how she felt. In the past, he would explain himself if he felt misunderstood. Now, it didn't matter as much. He often left her with little to no communication.

Sherice knew that leaving him would hurt him later because of their eleven-year friendship. They had been strictly friends who helped each other through all hardships and coached each other through all the games. For this reason, she wondered how he could leave her so freely. She tried to remind him of their friendship during the pain, but it was too late. She was crushed because although she didn't want to force the relationship, she never wanted to lose her friend.

Saying goodbye to ones she loves sent Sherice to dark places. She battled insecurity and depression, and she was left not wanting to do anything in life. It wasn't just because of Bernard's absence, but the fact that she lost herself while looking too deeply in the friendship and relationship. Bernard had disguised himself to be great, and she trusted him. Unfortunately, she later learned there was truth to the rumors she had heard about him. People said he was a liar, manipulator, verbal abuser, and a cheater who has a sex addiction that he denies. He is willing to do anything with any woman that had two legs, even if Sherice had satisfied him one-hour prior.

It hurt like hell to accept the truth. In fact, she tried to ignore the truth hoping that he could offer more than his cuteness, great body, and good sex. The two of them usually would chill during the week but turn up on weekends. They slept in many Sunday mornings. She was so caught up in the relationship that she didn't realize she had lost her way from church. One day, at different times, both of their mothers pushed them to get up and go to church. They hadn't mentioned church to them in a while, so Sherice felt that nudge to go.

Bernard rolled over and said, "Pray for me. I can't get up."

She grew so irritated with the thought that he could get up to party but couldn't get up to praise. Then, she heard his cough and realized he had come down with a cold. Unknowingly, she accepted another lie and went to church without him. When she walked into the church, she felt something come over her. The drinks from the night before that had her sluggish went away like a weight was lifted off her shoulders. When she got closer to the doors of the church, the hairs on her arm rose. It was like she was back in the presence of her first love.

The words in the sermon were powerful. The pastor spoke on the topic of obedience. It touched her spirit tremendously. As the first part of service ended, she decided she should get home because she promised to make Bernard some soup and tea and give him some meds to knock that cold out. However, before her body could move with her thoughts, the pastor who she never met called her out.

He said, "My daughter, I kept telling myself I'll speak to you after church, but I believe God wants me to talk to you now. When you sat down, I saw a light shine on you which lets me know the spirit already lives inside if you. Maybe you have lost your way for many reasons, but God wants you back!"

Sherice smiled but figured he was probably only saying that because she's a new face and that he might say that to anyone.

Then, he said, "The lady who prayed for you is my wife. When I saw you two standing on the side, God kept saying, my daughter. So, I knew you had a gift. As you were called on, I knew then the message to you was to move forward! I see you like a swan which is delicate. And, I see a head being chopped off, which is the head of the household or head of a church. As he showed me more of you, I saw a man. There's a man that's the head, and he's caused you so much pain, and God is not pleased."

As Sherice sat there, tears begin to roll because it was hitting home for her.

He said, "You were made to design, not only to design for family and friends, but I see you on a platform designing for the ministries. Be obedient. God will handle the rest. If not, He will come in a form that God doesn't want you to see. He will hurt you deeply, so get out while you can."

Sherice felt a mixture of relief and nervousness after hearing that message. She had so many mixed emotions. She felt so happy to receive such great confirmation. She felt amazing to have support. Sherice was so happy for that extra push even to go because the night before was extreme. As she left the church, her mind was going crazy. *How do I leave this man when we are on good terms?* How could she randomly turn her back now and not when her suspicions arose? She admitted to herself that bad things would happen if she didn't listen to the pastor, but it was easier said than done.

When she got in the house, his presence was so welcoming that it left her flesh weak. She thought about what the pastor said, but the way he held her in his arms felt so safe and warm. The look in his eyes made her feel so special. His smiles of missing her made her want to believe the pastor was just doing his job. But, deep down, she knew she couldn't convince herself. The message was too on point. As days passed, it seemed as if he was getting nicer. So, as she went for a drive to get food, her prayer changed.

She prayed, "God, how do I know that was you? If it was, why is it so hard to do as you said? Why is his behavior changing?"

A moment later, his lies hit the surface. A girl who had played her role claiming to be a friend turned out to be his sexual partner. The girls' relationship with Bernard had hit rock bottom, so her frustration allowed her to reach out to Sherice. Sherice wasn't surprised, so she didn't give the girl the satisfaction she wanted.

She responded, "I pray for healing in your time of need."

Sherice was surprised at her action. She asked herself, *"Why I didn't cuss her out? Why am I not angry? How could I be so dumb?"* She knew then that she wanted to leave. She just needed the push, and it was falling into her lap. That same night, she played it safe and even cuddled with him without letting him know she knew about the other woman. She had a headache later that night, so she laid down to rest. Her phone began to receive a text message. She saw them, but she didn't bother to check them. She would respond the next day.

When Sherice woke up, she realized she had a new message but not the ones from last night. She thought maybe she had been dreaming. She quickly remembered that she clears her data at night, but and this time messages were there. She realized that Bernard had gone through her phone. She was mad wondering why he was even doing that. It wasn't because she was doing anything. She wondered why he didn't trust her when he was the one living foully. She asked him about his searching, but she knew the type of person he was. She knew he would look her in the eyes with a straight face and tell a bold lie that came off so smoothly. He did just that.

Sherice knew who had messaged her the night before. So, she called the person to confirm, and they reassured that they did text her. His phone number had been tagged in the message, which was airing more of his dirty laundry. That's what made him erase the messages from her phone. Sherice wanted to know what the messages said, but the lady was heading into work. She couldn't talk at that moment, but there was something Bernard was avoiding.

As quickly as Sherice had heard that message in church, her relationship started falling apart. She realized she no longer had to wonder. Things were revealing themselves. If she didn't walk away from that relationship, she would've been a victim of something she'd wished she could have avoided. The same day she spoke to the woman on the phone about the messages, she went home and packed her bags with eyes filled with tears. The man that she loved was against her heart the entire time. It was time for her to love herself more.

Reminder:

The rear-view mirror of the car is for you to glance behind you from time to time. You use it to make sure there's nothing to block you from moving to the next lane. You even glance in it to avoid a rear-end crash. All the time you spend looking in the rearview mirror is less time spent focusing on what's in front of you. Stop looking in the rear view of your life when there's a beautiful scene before you. It's okay to see what's behind you from time to time to push and motivate you, remind you of what lane to not move to, and to watch out for the past coming full speed to stop you. God will give us all the power we need to get us through our days! Sometimes people should only be an assignment or a lesson in your life. However, we often confuse them for something greater, and we keep them around way longer than we should.

Don't make the mistakes Sherice did. When God told her not to pursue this guy, she got upset with questions like: *"God, you are so big. Why can't you change him and transform him into what I like? Why do I have to let go? It feels right. Why?"* It hurt her deeply to let go mentally because her flesh was attached to Bernard, but she knew with confirmation that spiritually he was no good for her! Sherice tried to be a man-builder and build up Bernard to be everything she wanted him to be. Meanwhile, he wasn't who God had for her. So, instead of her pulling back, she was only building him up for someone else to have him.

When God says stop, it might seem bad, but He has something greater that you can't see at that moment. You simply must let it go and let God have His way. Some days will be easier than others. Sometimes you will want to date again. Other times, you may even feel guarded, and that's okay. As time continues, the womb planted will be healed. Keep the faith and stay focused. As Sherice finally found the courage to stand up to the one that kept pushing her down, she had a foot out the door and told him she couldn't be in that relationship anymore. That was the moment she got her courage and strength back.

God blessed us with those instincts. He gave us small gut feelings that confirms the actions against us. We may not have the proof we need, but we have an intuition that won't steer us wrong. Sometimes we gain intuition from dealing with past situations. It's like a kid that reaches for a stove. Mommy says no, but he still wants to see why he isn't allowed to touch it. They must get burned to realize the pain of being disobedient. It is then that they realize they won't do that again. It takes experience and an open mind to gain wisdom. That is how you will discover what's right for you.

Question:

Have you ever ignored intuition? If so, how did it turn out for you?

_____

_____

_____

_____

_____

_____

_____

_____

Question:

What is your biggest fear in your current situation? Is it being single and entering the love life? Is it walking into a covenant (marriage) or getting over something that is not for you? Write your fear and then write a prayer asking God to give you clear direction.

_____

_____

_____

_____

_____

_____

_____

_____

Chapter 10

Did I Gain a Partner or Lost My Peace?

Genesis 2:24

"That is why a man leaves his father and mother and is united to his wife, and they become one flesh."

As the night skies dimmed the whole world, Darian gazed up glancing at the stars mesmerized with a clouded mind. Although she had so much on her mind, she felt empty. It was like her world had been filled with emotions that she couldn't quite feel. She became confused about what she should feel. Growing up, Darian heard stories of this feeling, but because it was not easily explained, she didn't quite understand until she felt it. It's not like you're angry or even happy. It's like you're zoned out into the world of thought. You almost feel safe but also alone.

But God...

For so long, Darian thought to herself, *"Wow, that girl is gorgeous."* She stood admiring every detail of the woman's beauty. She wasn't just impressed with the exterior appearance. She also admired the strength that defined her. Her confidence made her different from most. Other women look at the next woman as competition, but it was something about her that made her unique. Darian glanced in the mirror and silently thought these things about herself. She truly admired the woman in the mirror.

For years, Darian took jab after jab mentally, spiritually, and emotionally. After dealing with abandonment and feeling unwanted from family, friends, and even while dating, she had no problem dismissing things that no longer served her purpose. Although that was a good idea and seemed easy to do, it triggered pain deep within her. Somehow this woman fiercely fought back the tears after every trial. She fixed her dress and stormed through everything that was meant to break her down. She didn't believe in letting anyone see her down. She felt if she showed vulnerability by allowing anyone to see her weakness, it gave them the power to control her mind or self-esteem. Darian was that young lady that couldn't allow her mind to consume such confusion.

On January 2nd, after a day of fun festivities, Darian slept in bed late and rejuvenated from every cup of alcohol she'd consumed. Her head pounded double the bass of the music repeating in her thoughts. Her makeup was smeared on her face as she had no strength to properly wash it off the night before. She had an amazing time escaping everything she endured the previous year. As she heard the wind swish through the leaves giving her a breath of fresh air, she inhaled. Her stomach began to growl, and she knew she needed to get up and get something to eat.

As she stood to her feet nice and tall, her head felt heavy. Darian felt like someone took two bags of large rocks and placed them on the crown of her head. She grabbed the bottle of water from her nightstand and took a few sips. Then, she walked over to her dresser and grabbed her face towel to wash the makeup off. Hopefully, the heat from the warm shower would help remove it. She made way to the restroom and turned on the hot water. Then, she began to splash her face. As Darian used washed off her makeup, she began to frown. The lady she thought was gorgeous looked back at her in the mirror and didn't appear to be so beautiful anymore.

Darian's reality kicked in, and she no longer had the strength to keep fixing her dress and storming forward. She once admired her confidence and strength as she defeated all odds and adversities against her. Deep down, she didn't realize that cutting people off and continuing to push forward was causing her world to become smaller. She began to view her life realistically, and it felt miserable. She allowed herself to be broken and handle herself as such. She popped bottles of alcohol in hopes that she could enjoy the night and forget everything. She laughed hard to keep herself from being an emotional drinker. She danced all night ignoring the dizziness that came over her. She thought she handled herself well when she wasn't even living in her truth. Or, was she?

She didn't know who she was anymore. She was overwhelmed at the idea of her fellow Christian brothers and sisters judging her ways of handling depression, the youth who idolized her, and even the people who didn't believe in her or thought she simply wasn't good enough. She molded her character with a mask trying to impress everyone from every angle. Nevertheless, she didn't impress the one that matters – God. She felt ashamed and hurt thinking that God would no longer accept her. She thought her mistakes over the years wouldn't be forgiven.

Darian lowered the toilet seat lid and sat down to regroup. Standing too long wasn't a great idea. A heat wave came over her body, and her mouth got clouded as if she was getting ready to vomit. She didn't want that, so she tried everything she could to avoid it. As reality set in, she began to cry. She didn't want to accept who she was becoming, but her old ways were fading, and she couldn't figure out how to get back to that place she once was. She didn't know if she even wanted to go there.

Friends she thought were her biggest supporters gossiped about her. She didn't have a problem with their opinion. However, the pain came because they always spoke behind her back. When the information got to Darian, it came out negatively. Relationships were not the best for her. She couldn't find the perfect one to compliment her. The family shared more about her down times and often played the guessing game on what was next in her life. She couldn't trust anyone. So, when moments of depression kicked in, she handled them alone to protect the little peace she did have. Darian decided to go back to bed. She couldn't stand long enough to make anything to eat. All she wanted to do was lay down. She was back in bed resting when she received a phone call from her friend Shanell.

"Hey, Girly. What's up?"

"Happy New Year, Shuga!" Shanell said in full excitement.

"Hey, Hun. Same to you," Darian said in a sluggish tone.

Shanell couldn't help but ask what was wrong. As Darian paused and thought, she had a million things cross her mind in only seconds. However, she could only fix her lips to mumble a few words.

"Nothing. Just tired."

Shanell felt something was wrong, but she didn't bother pressing the issue. She knew that if it were too bad, Darian would share if needed. When Darian realized the conversation wasn't intriguing her mind, she told Shanell that she would call her when she woke up. She got off the phone and began to shut her eyes, but another call came in. She looked at her phone and contemplated if she should answer or not. The name "No Liar Zone" on her screen confused her on how to respond. Her mind said, *"Don't you dare answer the phone,"* but her heart was yearning to hear his voice. This was her most recent boyfriend, Marcus, that she was trying to leave alone. The two of them spent many nights together. Although she'd had a few drinks, she knew that he was acting suspiciously when she called and texted him the night before. The moment she went to answer the call, the phone stopped ringing. Seconds later, the phone rang again. This time, she decided that not answering would be best, so she didn't. Shannell knew something strange was going on, but she wasn't sure if she was ready to know what could be the unknown.

Two months ago…

It was eight o'clock on a Monday night. Darian grabbed some grapes and apple juice, turned the channel to VH1, and tuned in to her favorite ratchet T.V. show, *Love and Hip Hop*. It was the reunion episode. The cast started calmly until someone got rowdy and the roles drastically switched. The cast was ready to fight. As much as she tried to stop watching reality tv shows, Darian couldn't resist. In the next room, her boyfriend, Marcus, was playing his PS4 and listening to music on the speaker. They were both fully occupied for the next few hours.

Usually, when the reality shows were on, he would either watch the sports games, work out, or play the video game online.

As one of the reality stars started explaining her pain of dealing with the heartbreak of her man sleeping with the other reality star, Marcus was yelling at the screen of his game. Darian could not stand when he would get that loud, but she didn't bother addressing it because she was satisfied that he was home. When the show went to commercial, she decided to kiss and hug Marcus goodnight because her eyes were heavy. She loved having him home because every time he was with his boys, he never had a mind of his own and was easily influenced by their actions.

Darian retreated to her room and continued watching T.V. Marcus continued to enjoy his evening. After a while, he realized the tone of his voice, the music, and the game were getting louder. He lowered the volume and then went to check on Darian. He noticed she had dozed off, so he kissed her goodnight and went back into the room and closed the door behind him. The music paused briefly, and coincidentally, Marcus yelled to the game at the same time. His voice woke Darian up, and she started watching what was on TV. She looked at the clock, noticed thirty minutes passed.

The music paused again, and Marcus yelled, "Come on, man!" An incoming call was interrupting the music and distracting him from the game. He answered and placed the caller on speaker. The walls were thin enough for Darian to hear the conversation word for word. It was his mom calling. She asked what he was doing, how was his day and did he go to work today. He answered everything short because he was so tuned in to the game. His mom went silent for a moment, so he asked did she go to her treasure meeting for church. She responded that she didn't, and he resumed playing his game and started yelling at the players again.

His mom waited for him to get silent and asked, "What are you getting me for the holidays?"

Darian and Marcus splurged the year prior on Christmas gifts. Since they were investing in other things with little to no help, they weren't doing it big in the gift department this year. It made much sense to the both of them, so they agreed collectively.

With that in mind, he responded, "I'm not doing much this year. I'm only shopping for the kids and Darian."

She instantly said, "Oh heck no. I come before all of them."

He laughed and said, "That's my lady."

His mom said, "So! You two are not married yet."

He said, "And, the kids are my siblings."

"Like I said, I come before all of them."

Darian's skin started boiling. *So, this is what you say or think when I'm not around. Is it a slight competition for you?* She was confused. She understood that no one was perfect, but the way his mother spoke was heartfelt. Those kids weren't hers. They were her ex-husband's kids. Marcus's mother didn't care about Darian or those kids. That bothered Darian because she loved her as if she were her mom. Marcus knew his mom wasn't right.

He laughed and said, "Chill. I'm getting something for Kelly, too"

Kelly is his niece and her granddaughter. His mom paused and laughed.

"Yea, her too," she said to smooth the conversation.

At this point, Darian turned on some music and tried to go back to sleep. Although he told his mom to chill, his laughter gave her room to keep saying inappropriate things. It made Darian view her differently, so she decided she would keep her distance going forward.

No one knew the plans Darian had put together for both of their parents with her bonus check. It was truly a heartfelt gift because she thought their relationship was good. Against her agreement with Marcus, she bought tickets for them to see some of the top gospel singers perform. However, she had canceled it because of how much his mother's words hurt her. She thought, *why waste money on someone who views me in that way?* She wanted to be her daughter-in-law, not compete over her son. It was unfortunate because Marcus had to attend future family events without her. It was almost as if he had to choose. That eventually put a strain on Marcus and Darian's relationship. It became difficult for him. So, he had to address his mother.

Even then, Marcus's mother still didn't see where it went wrong. At that point, Darian felt disappointed in the way she heard her speak behind her back. Nevertheless, she agreed to disagree and decided to move forward. However, Darian learned that his mother called his family asking their input instead of calling her future daughter-in-law to get clarity and come to common ground. She got more people involved when the misunderstanding could have been fixed. Instead, it was only getting worse. Others' opinions, comments, and concerns interfered and only fueled the fire. That made Darian uncomfortable with everyone.

As the days, weeks, and months went on, Darian forgave his mother without an apology, but the tension never really faded. She started noticing changes in her relationship with Marcus because she didn't want to be around his family. They weren't bonding like old times. He even changed his daily patterns even though they always said no one could ever come between them. Darrian couldn't believe that his actions were not only allowing family but even friends to break their promise. As she pondered the situation, she started to feel abandoned by Marcus. Furthermore, she was upset that he didn't defend her as she had wished he would.

Marcus grew distant and began to engage more in outside activities to avoid Darian. With tears in her eyes, she wondered why he would give her false hope. She had never been so vulnerable. He began making promises he could barely remember. They were covered deeply in all his lies. He made her believe she meant everything to him. Darian wished and prayed for him to become better. She wanted him to make something more of himself in the relationship. He left her no choice but to pull back because he hurt her. He cut her in a way no other man could because he was first her best friend. She'd already feared crossing that path, but her heartbeat big for him, so she felt he was worth the try. For that reason, she could not understand how he could claim to love her, but as soon as he got upset, he would run so far away from her physically, spiritually, and emotionally.

As time passed, his tone became rough, his attitude became strong, his moods were negative, and his gentle touch became aggressive. Darian knew the relationship was shifting, but it was hard for her to accept it. She was everything a man could want in a woman but dealing with Marcus made her feel the emptiest. She walked away from the relationship so freely as she does with anyone else. So, she wondered why her heart yearned for his love. As much as she hated him for lying, manipulating, and cheating, her heart wouldn't allow her to let go.

Darian didn't get what he could be calling for two months later. She was drunk, depressed, and hurt, but she couldn't allow him into her darkest days. As the weeks passed, Darian had felt no different from how she felt on New Year's Day. Normally, she would be motivated to conquer the year, but this year was a stretch. Darian woke up bright and early without an alarm to make her way to church. She had gospel music blasting as she got ready. Her mood was down, but surprisingly her spirit was lifted. All she could think about was receiving a positive message to help push forward. As she continued to be obedient and stayed focused, her business began to flourish. Her health was in tack, her lifestyle made sense, and her connections were more spiritual. Her life became peaceful, and she couldn't believe her confidence was increasing over time. Her newfound friendships were developing and evolving. Moreover, her spiritual growth had blossomed.

She no longer chased her ex-boyfriend. Her king found her and directed her to Proverbs 18:22 "He who finds a wife finds a good thing." Darian finally realized that she mattered to someone other than herself. She was happy, and no longer had to hide behind a mask. Darian developed growth and maturity from circumstances and situations. She followed the plan of the Lord which led her to the fulfillment of happiness - something no man on earth can fulfill.

Reminder:

It wasn't until Darian allowed herself to be vulnerable in the right place that she could receive a great understanding on how to overcome her setbacks. It took a lot of sacrificing to leave. In some cases, the 21-day detox is good for helping you get into the right place with God. Fasting for twenty-one days is helpful because that's how much time it takes to break a habit. After the fast, you will feel rejuvenated, and your intuition will be fully functional.

When your intuition tells you something or someone isn't right, watch the fruit and move accordingly. Try not to allow your feelings to manifest. Doing so will cause the result to be worse than it has to be. Also, please forgive yourself for the mistakes you made. Repent and ask God to forgive you and move forward. Taking time to shame and bash yourself can lead you to make poor choices creating more sin. Making mistakes is okay. Just try your very best not to repeat it. Do not focus on the Negative Nancy's and the Nasty Naysayers. They will talk, so give them something positive to say. Continue to work on yourself and become a better you daily.

Parents, when your prince or princess begins to date, be mindful that you once were where they were. You are not losing a child but gaining an additional member to your family (if they last). Even if the relationship does not work out, he or she has gained experience as you did. You can't raise the other children, but prayerfully you raised yours to the best of your ability to be all that you prayed for them to be. Your decisions of judgment can take a toll on one or both parties. It leaves your child to make difficult choices; it doesn't mean you will lose a place in their life at all. No one can ever take that place. You are simply allowing them to grow and learn from their decisions.

In this world, temptation is a challenge. Getting caught up in the wrong things is easier. Misery loves company, and it finds ways to damage homes and hearts. Not every person your child brings into your space will receive an open approval. Nevertheless, allow them to learn just as you had to do when you were their age. At some point, we must grow up and learn to co-exist so that it doesn't put a strain and stress on your child's health.

The outsiders that are against the couple are more than enough stress. Couples need support, especially from the parents. As a father, you are the first man that your daughter loves. She looks to you on what to accept from other men. Women, you are the first lady your son sees. The way you carry yourself helps him to develop a great eye when choosing his rib. Be the best example for your kids so it won't be hard for you to accept their soulmate when they choose their loves. Most importantly, pray them through it, and trust that even if it's not the best choice, they learn something from it that will mature their character.

Question:

Have you ever battled with the thoughts of your significant other having to choose you or their parents?

_____

_____

_____

_____

_____

_____

_____

_____

_____

_____

_____

_____

_____

_____

_____

_____

_____

_____

_____

_____

_____

_____

_____

_____

_____

Chapter 11

How to Move on When a Person Reveals Their Truth

Isaiah 59:19

"When the enemy coming in like a flood, the Spirit of the Lord will lift up a standard against him."

Ronnell came home to bring his little sister, Janell, to see Karen. They laughed and talked.

As they got ready to go, Karen asked, "What do you all have planned?"

"We are going to the park," Janell said full of excitement.

It was about eighty degrees out with a nice breeze. Although Karen thought it was a great day to get out, she never received an invite, so she stayed tucked in bed relaxing. Ronnell made Janell go to the restroom before leaving. She put her toys down ran to the bathroom as instructed.

"Is everything okay?" Ronnell asked Karen.

She responded, "Yes, I'm okay, but I need to talk to you. I feel sick, and I'm not sure why."

He smiled and said, "You think you might be pregnant?"

She stretched and said, "My body hasn't been normal. Do you mind getting a test while you're out?"

He responded sarcastically, "Of course."

Deep inside Karen, was praying she wasn't pregnant. She knew he was ready. However, she would be stuck trying to raise a baby that he did not want. As

Ronnell got ready to ask Karen something, Janell came back to the room.

"I'm ready," she said.

"Well let's get to pushing," Ronnell replied.

They hugged and kissed Karen and left her side as she rolled over in bed with a headache and fever. She felt like she could be catching the flu, but she wanted to weigh all options. With a headache becoming so intense and feeling like a migraine, she decided to take a nap. While she was resting, her phone rung three times and disrupted her sleep. It was her friend Shayla calling to cry about the heartbreak she had just experienced. Karen wanted to be there for her friend, but her body wasn't allowing her to do so. So, she kept her eyes closed. She was half asleep while she listened with little to no response back.

All she could remember hearing was, "Just call when you wake up."

Karen apologized and said, "I'll call when I get up. I'm so tired."

They ended the conversation, but Karen's sleep was broken, and she couldn't get back to sleep. She logged on to her social media and saw a picture posted of Ronnell and Janell. She commented on how cute they were and wished she could've been there. As she ran to the restroom once again, she had a major urge to pee with little to nothing releasing from her body. She wondered what was wrong with her. She went back to the room and laid down. When she picked her phone back up, his picture was the first thing on her newsfeed, but she noticed her comment had been deleted. She was disturbed by this, but she still didn't bother to ask why.

Later that night, Ronnell posted a Throwback Thursday photo of himself in a suit. Karen couldn't help but to love that picture and admire how it would be when they got married. He quickly deleted that comment as well. Karen picked the phone up so quickly and dialed his number.

Before he could answer, she was asking, "What is your issue? What are you trying to hide by deleting everything I post on your page?"

He responded, "Here you go starting stuff again. I deleted everyone's comment not just yours."

Ronnell and Karen had been together five years, so she knew any sudden changes he made. He had over two hundred pictures. He saved every memory possible. She knew something wasn't right; she just didn't know what it was. Karen couldn't help but to go through his photos and see if she noticed anything. She saw one girl who commented on every picture. Her name was Jonay, and she put heart eyes and lustful comments as if she was interested in Ronnell.

Karen was taught never to attack the women. She didn't attack; she just had questions because she noticed the disrespect. Karen's pictures are all over his account, so Jonay knew he was in a relationship. And, it was clear she didn't care. Karen knew in her heart she would look crazy addressing the female, but her hands wouldn't stop typing.

"Good afternoon, Jonay. I don't even like being in this position of allowing myself to look weak. However, as I've noticed Ronnell isn't going to admit anything. I am not coming at you with any disrespect, messiness, or drama. So, as a woman, not only coming for a man but healthwise, coming to ask do you and him have something going on?"

Jonay's response was immature as Karen expected. She made jokes of Karen's insecurities. It was sad that

Ronnell would even put Karen in this position. He was supposed to protect her, not have anyone laughing at her. He saw no wrong in it, except for Karen's actions. He shamed her on how stupid and dumb she was. The young lady told Karen it was nothing between them and she needed to check her insecurities. She also suggested that Karen stop following Ronnell on social media, so she wouldn't get offended on what he posted. Karen was done responding. She couldn't give Jonay any more than she already did, so she left everything alone.

A week later, Karen woke up feeling anxious. She battles with anxiety. She called her neighbor whose boyfriend is close friends with Ronnell. She wanted to see if she could locate him. Her friend could barely help her situations, so she didn't want to get involved in theirs. Karen learned then that every friend in your life is for a reason so that she couldn't expect much more from the neighbor. Meanwhile, she couldn't ignore the fact that her treasure box was itching and on fire. She had been having an unusual period for longer than a week. *"What STD did this man give me? I've only been with him,"* she thought. She rushed to the hospital to get checked immediately.

As Karen got to the hospital, the doctor ask was she pregnant. She quickly said, "No… Well, I don't know. I hope not. The doctor gave her a cup to obtain a urine sample. When she got to the bathroom, she could barely pee. She had the urge, but nothing would come out. She did what she could. When she got back to the room, they stuck her with an IV. As she awaited her test results, she constantly called around in search for her boyfriend. She wanted him to be there, but he was nowhere to be found. She called her neighbor again and told her what was happening. Her neighbor asked if she was lying. They felt she wanted attention. Karen wondered how they could challenge her character. What type of support was that? Karen was hurt. The doctor came in and shared the test results.

"You were dehydrated. The itch isn't an STD. It was a bacterial infection which can come from a variety of things."

He also informed Karen that she was not pregnant. She thought the news of not being pregnant would excite her, but hearing her minor illness became heartbreaking. She couldn't believe her ears as she stared at the walls feelings like they were closing in on her. The information was small, but Karen knew in her heart that the infection had to come from Ronnell. Karen called Ronnell repeatedly but had no luck. She felt alone. When she got home, information came to her that night that had been at the movies with Jonay. Something happened between Ronnell and Jonay that made her upset enough to tell Karen.

Jonay messaged Karen pictures of her and Ronnell at the park the same day he left her house with his little sister. She sent screenshots of them planning to get a room and meet each other. They went to the movies with Ronnell's friends who were also in Karen's life. Karen was hurt, but it was what she expected. She just didn't want to hear it. This girl played her role, and they laughed at Karen as if she was the crazy one. They were wrong though. She was no fool, and her intuition was screaming. However, her pain wouldn't let this go so smoothly.

Karen knew Jonay's boyfriend and shared every screenshot with him. She thought she was wrecking one home when she was wrecking her own. She had been dating her boyfriend for eight years. Because he was away in school, she was bored and decided to talk to other people. She kept announcing how she could hurt Karen's feelings, but she hurt her own more. Jonay cried her eyes out to her boyfriend stating Karen was lying, but the screenshots couldn't lie. She felt stupid, and all the insecurities she claimed Karen possessed were the ones she battled with the most.

Karen sent her a message saying, *"I never intended for either of us to get hurt, but because you took this to the next level, you, unfortunately, had to reap the harvest that you sowed. No hard feelings to you, but I pray you seek guidance on how to cope. You are hurt and have been hurt. You thought it was okay to hurt someone else. I would be crazy to go to someone else's home and do this because I experienced it. I'm praying for you."*

Leaving her no room to respond with negativity, Karen then blocked her. She sat in silence with her music on full blast she replayed the situation. She was mad at the world but found it funny how everything played out. She also tried to stay humble because the battle wasn't over. She heard the door shut, so she turned the music down a few notches. Ronnell came into the bedroom and stood at the door. He was mesmerized. Karen had on a black lace bra and panties set. He walked up behind her holding and kissing on her.

With anger boiling but loving his gentle lips and touch, she delivered the news of what she knew. She was tired of trying to figure out the best way to say it.

She blurted out, "You like Jonay, I see. Be with her. This is over."

He simply said it was false. Karen reached over to get her phone. She went first to the messages that showed his number and then to the pictures of the family day at the park. As he grabbed his stuff, in her head she wanted him to leave, but she also wanted answers.

He kept saying, "She's lying only to make you mad, and you're falling for it."

With tears in her eyes, she knew the truth. She had the truth. There was no argument needed. But, how could he? How could he break her heart? Karen had just shared with him that she was possibly pregnant, and he still didn't turn down that date to the park.

As she watched him get his stuff, she said, "Don't take half of your things. Get it all."

He said, "You just need to cool down."
It was disrespectful of him thinking this could just blow over, but he was not even willing to explain what the hell was going on. She walked behind him.

"Ronnell! Why must you..." Karen yelled while running down the stairs, chasing behind him. "How could you?"

Ronnell's prideful ways gave her little to no conversation.

"Go in the house, Karen."

As her eyes filled with tears, she looked at him and said, "Really?"

God revealed to her what she needed to know. Her heart was weakened and didn't know how to move forward with that information. She loved him deeply, and the betrayal she felt was unexplainable. He started the car up and tried to speed off, but that mission failed. He lowered the window.

"Go in the house. I don't feel like talking."

The car shut off right after he told her that. Before this, he had no car troubles. He was furious that it was happening now. He couldn't run from his problems anymore. He tried to turn the car back on to let window up. As he attempted to do that, Karen smiled and walked away.

"God, I see you," she said. "I'm out the way."

Ronnell said, "You always think it's because of you that I'm punished, or God allows things to happen."

Without a drizzle warning, the rain began to pour. Ronnell was so upset. His night couldn't get any worse. It was storming outside, but he dreaded walking in that storm to go in the house. He stayed in the car on the phone as he called a tow truck. Karen continued to clean up her house and remove the negativity. She was done with being a doormat to someone she loved.

Reminder:

Don't chase a partner that's running from you. We all have a choice. Some choose to play games. Others are ready to settle down. If a person wants to leave, allow them to do so. In most cases, when you beg and force them to move against their heart's decisions, you jeopardize your own heart. You would then have to accept false love. You must pay attention to their actions and move accordingly. Like Karen, I☐ believe we all have made some long-term commitments that should've been short-seasoned. I'll be the first to admit that I have been hard-headed in my past as well. If I can recall having many signs telling me to let it go during those times. Whether it was a pastor in his sermon, a message from someone random, or even a message on a kids' cartoon show, I☐ ignored it! I thought I was over analyzing my life and not living it.

Just like Karen, you must realize that the warning signs are not always negative individuals who are trying to break you down. Sometimes God will use anyone or anything to deliver a message to you. If the actions of your mate seem unpleasant, ask God to provide you strength to make the best decisions. The last thing you want to do is be stuck in a place that God released from your life. I can honestly say that finding closure is not easy. One of the worse feelings to have when deciding to leave is depression. It's like you can't eat, breath, or sleep without them because you yearn for your request of love in them.

Know that God will start to reveal the truth even if it hurts. At that point, you may not even care anymore because your heart has shut down. Understand that I am not encouraging prideful behavior. Go after love if it's genuine and heaven sent. Sometimes making decisions when you're mad can bring bad judgment and possible mistakes like when you are running after someone whose actions have proven how much they didn't want to be committed. Find strength, wash your hands, and throw in the towel. You are stronger when you realize your self-worth. Stop allowing people to use and abuse you. Moreover, stop fighting for something that no longer serves a purpose in your life.

Question:

Have you ever had to deal with "the other one?" How did you handle it?

_____

_____

_____

_____

_____

_____

_____

Chapter 12

Will It Ever Get Better After Making Me Bitter?

Ephesians 4:31

"Let all bitterness and wrath and anger and clamor and slander be put away from you, along with malice."

A couple of years ago, Remy's life was so busy that she had to write down her daily agenda. She had so much on her to do list one day that she doubted she would be able to accomplish all. She and her fiancé argued about spending time together. She wanted to go on a date, but he had already made plans to ride his bike and go to the bar with his friends. Remy didn't like to isolate herself, but she tried to stay out of trouble, so she preferred to be a homebody for respect.

Remy was leaving work on Tuesday, October 18, 2016. She had to make wedding arrangements. Usually, before she drives, she would say a short prayer. This day, she got in the car, grabbed a piece of Double Mint gum, turned her song up, and took off. *BOOM!* In only a matter of seven minutes max, Remy had gotten into an accident. When everyone hears someone had an accident, they think of the money that comes from it. However, at that moment, it was not about the money, the argument earlier, or the dinner that was prepping. It was the fear of life or death. Being in a car alone during that time made the experience even more terrifying.

Nevertheless, God woke that couple up to remind them that things can turn around so fast, so to cherish each moment. Remy's fiancé, Domo, was first on the scene. He had heard in her voice that she was not okay. As much as she was grateful for him being there, she was more concerned about what she should do next. Her adrenaline was rushing, her mind was racing, and the fear of it all overpowered her.

Remy watched as the tow truck drove off with her wrecked vehicle. Tears filled her eyes. She couldn't believe her car was totaled that fast. It wasn't about the material possession. It was just the thought that it's time to slow down. She felt her fiancé was living too fast, not her. Remy was on the road a lot for work, bible study, church gatherings, ladies' night, visiting family, and then back home. For her to be young, her life seemed fun, but her days were filled with business. The wreck was a heartbreaking moment. She had to accept the fact that her world was crashing. There was a lesson in this, but she couldn't really figure out what it could be.

When Domo jammed a toe, Remy didn't miss a scream. If he hurt himself in sports, Remy pushed him to get checked. She valued every detail of him and his life as if it was her own. She noticed that when they were in the hospital that night, he had a face of frustration. She couldn't tell why. So, she suggested that they go home.

He said, "No, I'm just tired."

As much as she wanted to accept his answer, his body language made her feel discomfort.

"Please, can we leave?" she asked the doctor.

The doctor replied, "I suggest you stay. There is a cut on your liver. This could be a life or death situation. You would need to continue to be watched."

"Whoa! What?"

Remy didn't like the sound of death in the same sentence as her name. She sat back and started to pray.

When she started to cry, Domo came over, held her hand and sung her favorite song. He can't sing, but it was special.

As time drew near for her to discharge, Remy spoke with her Aunt Peaches. Peaches offered to help later in the day so that Domo could rest for work. Domo and Remy agreed that her parents could watch her during the day while he's at work. The plan sounded cool until she came on her cycle a few days later. She just wanted to shower and get settled in the comfort of her own home. She explained this to Domo.

He said, "Well, you need to wait because I'm going out with the guys tonight."

Remy replied, "No, you're not. I'm always here for you, and nothing comes before. So why are you shutting me down now that I'm telling you I need you?"

"I'm not shutting you down. I'm telling you I'll be there later two or three in the morning."

Those hours are disrespectful to her parents' home.

He yelled and said, "You are in the way! You don't think this is affecting me, too?"

That selfish bastard had the nerve to make her feel like nothing after everything she had done for him. It wasn't because he was going out. It was the fact that she asked for something, which she barely does, and got shut down. However, the moment a pin drops, she's running to pick it up for him.

That night, he came to get her. As they drove, she was already afraid because of her accident. He drove 80-mph in the 50-mph zone. He trailed cars closely. Not to mention, when she got in the accident, she hit the side of her face which affected her eardrum. Knowing this, he still blasted the music. With tears coming down - and not just the silent cry - but that cry a four-year-old does when you spank them - was her reaction to the way he was behaving. He didn't care to slow down or chill out. All he cared about was that she was stopping him from his fun.

It was then that she realized she gives more to people than they give to her. Remy did everything on her own and poured so much into everyone, especially Domo. She didn't leave room to see how he would do if the roles changed. So, this was that opportunity to know who was for her and against her. It was a time for her to see who used her because she was convenient and who really loved her.

Remy had enough of the way he treated her. The complaints stopped. She knew his truth. Ironically, a week and a half later, Domo got thrown off his bike.

He said with a smile, "Yo, that car almost crushed me."

She responded, "That's not funny."

He said, "I wasn't laughing. I'm saying it's crazy.

Unfortunately, he still didn't learn the lesson. Life can switch in a blink of an eye, so cherish the relationships surrounding you. Some people aren't given a second or third chance. The moment she started to tell Domo that God didn't like how he was at that time and she felt it was a wakeup call, he didn't like the response. Remy remained down for several months. Domo would drop her off to work five-minutes away every morning, and she would take an Uber home in the evening. She was cool with that. The lesson was about the relationship they had. It was a wakeup call to see how much she protected him and how much he failed to make her feel protected.

In his mind, because he sped on his bike to her the day of the wreck was more than enough. The vows said "in sickness and health," so for as long as she's down he was supposed to be right there beside her like he was when she was up. There was no excuse!

A year later, God blessed Remy with a brand new 2017 truck with only three miles on it. She left the lot paying the same amount she was paying for a car. God wanted her to see how rough it could get, but if she never loses sight and trusts Him through the process, He will work it out. Full of excitement, Remy sent the picture of her new truck to Domo. He asked what kind it was. She told him, and he simply said, "Oh okay. I'm heading to my sister's house for her birthday dinner."

She sent the same picture to her friends, and everyone responded with excitement. *"Congratulations! He pulled you through!"* While she was at the dealership, she ran into her ex-boyfriend, Jeremiah. He overheard her discussing her excitement to the seller. Jeremiah looked so amazed.

"Remy, you are so blessed to be here and share your testimony. I would've never known. You don't look like what you've been through."

Remy shook her head and said, "BUT GOD."

She began to think to herself. He was saying she didn't look messed up physically. Imagine what she feels emotionally and mentally from the man in her life.

"You don't even realize how much you just inspired me. You are just going to walk off the lot showing out like that?" he said jokingly. "That car is not even ready for you. You deserve that and more. Although you don't understand it now, He worked it out for what He's getting ready to do in your life."

Remy got into her brand-new ride, and tears started flowing. She read the messages again. She wondered why Domo only said, "Oh okay." It just didn't seem right. It almost seems like they were enemies or opponents. Where's the *"You can do it, baby. You got this?"* Where's the pat on the back? Sometimes he just wasn't as genuine as she would have wished for him to be. He claimed to be in love. It just doesn't look like it. His actions were screaming louder than his words. It shook her mood to hear another man say what she wanted to hear from her man. Nonetheless, she couldn't let it get the best of a happy moment. *"Even though the relationship may not ever get better, especially if it's confirmed they are not for you, God can still work out other things that are greater for you,"* she thought.

Long ago, Remy was very low-key. She didn't accept the dating lifestyle. Her focus was on school, working, dancing, saving, and building her platform for her future. When she finally started dating, she met a guy named Jeremiah. He was perfectly described as her crush. His smile was perfectly straight and pearly white. His hair was curly and soft. He had milk chocolate skin with no rashes or bumps. This man had the look down to the T and the personality that wins every heart.

Remy would stare at him in a daze as he walked passed her. She would build so much confidence to talk about him when he wasn't around, but the moment he came near her, she would shut down. One day she was properly introduced to him. Her heart raced as he walked over to her. Jeremiah looked so confident and well put together. She was praying inside that she didn't look as crazy as her heart and mind were going.

Although that was the start of what could now be something special, it didn't go anywhere beyond a friendship. At the time, he was brave enough to inform her that the player inside of him wasn't any good for her. He saw Remy's heart and knew what she wanted. It took him some time to see and understand what she meant by different. Remy wasn't on him like the other girls. They would throw their bodies at him. However, she just wasn't the girl that was going for that.

As the time passed, conversation decreased. Still, when things came about, they always showed support for each other. When times would get hard, they would know to call and check on each other to be that voice of relief the other needed. It didn't matter which one was down, the other would say, "Come on, best friend. Let's go to church." It was very confusing how they could be best friends, but the flesh had an attachment. It was nothing like having someone around that's your boo and your best friend.

Remy and Jeremiah could tell the ins, outs, ups, and downs of every situation they entered with no judgment. She knew about the games he played. He was one of her teachers from a man's view. She never allowed anybody to take advantage because he taught her what not to accept. He was gentle to women's emotions because of the advice Remy instilled in him. Each man's life that Remy entered, their mother saw something good in her. In this case, not only did his momma see it but the whole crew knew.

They could stay up until sunrise just talking and couldn't even tell time was moving. There wasn't any faking, covering up, putting on a mask, or pretending. They kept it real and laid their stories on the line. It didn't matter if one felt something as small as their right butt cheek itching or something as big as filing bankrupt. There was nothing too embarrassing to share. No flaw, life changes, significant other could scare the connection away. It was just too impossible. They were not good for each other, so that was the least of anyone's worries, but they were never good apart!

After talking for hours when they would separate or disconnect the phone, an hour or so later, one of them called with more stories as if they missed out on years. The type of vibe they shared was like they could hang out with each other like homies, have each other's backs like family, be prayer partners like the church, be voices of encouragement like their parents, check each other's wrongdoings quickly like their siblings, listen like best friends, and maintain a physical connection like a boo thang. This one relationship had always been uniquely defined. No one could quite understand it, not even them.

One day, the relationship became more intense. That was frightening for both. They couldn't allow their true lives to hurt the other, so they had to pull back so that they never lost the friendship. They went off to start dating other people. In those years, Jeremiah always looked for Remy in each woman but couldn't find her. Remy also tried to take the skills she learned from Jeremiah and enter it into her relationships, but no one could match it. That's why their relationship was unique.

As much as they wanted to be friends as Remy embarked a new chapter in her life with someone else, it was impossible! Everything would be compared, or Domo would feel disrespected as anyone would. If Remy saw Domo associating with his ex-girlfriend, she would have cut him off. However, while Remy was coming out of a storm in her current relationship, it felt good for her to see Jeremiah and feel something positive after not seeing each other for some time. Having a friend of the opposite sex can become a huge issue. The moment your significant other messes up, the human mind will start to reach out or reminisce about an ex-boyfriend or girlfriend. That's not fair to your current relationship. So, no matter how much Remy wanted to catch up and see Jeremiah again, she couldn't.

Reminder:

Don't allow your situation to minimize your concentration. Don't lose faith in God's commandments and fall short within your circumstances. Keep God beside you always. More importantly, He needs to be inside you spiritually. When you lose sight of God and stray from keeping Him first in relationships, it's bound to go downhill. With God in the midst, it will get better for you whether you have the heart to leave or even if you choose to fight and stay. He gives us free will to make choices. Only you know how much you can take in any relationship with family, friends, or lovers. If you focus on putting your trust into God and not man, you will see He is the comforter. He has your back forever and always.

If you are done with someone, be done. Remy had not left the relationship with Domo. So, no matter how much she loved Jeremiah's words, she could not engage deeper. When you break up with someone, you don't have to hate them or bash them. You don't even have to let the world know there's trouble in paradise. Sometimes when you are in a storm like Remy faced, God wants your attention. It doesn't mean it's time to find the next person to date. It doesn't even mean that you have to call all your homegirls to feed your mind with their opinion. Simply look to God to see where He needs you. If Remy had taken the bait of Jeremiah's charming words, she would not have known if had motives when he heard her testimony. She did not know Jeremiah's position in life nor did she know if the devil himself didn't send him at the perfect time to distract her in her vulnerability. For this reason, it is best just to stay focused.

If you run into an ex, I believe you can greet them if you're not on bad terms. However, if you are still weak for that person or they are weak for you, there's nothing left to say. Keep walking! Don't allow them a space of comfort for no reason to jeopardize your next relationship. Give that new relationship a fair shot and the security it deserves. Your mate is not insecure if they don't want you in contact with your ex. It is disrespectful for you not to end the relationship with the ex if you are truly trying to commit. Take it from me. In a few of my past relationships, I've dealt with the battles of so many women in my significant other's life that I couldn't distinguish which ones were tricky friends versus the ones that wanted more. You can never truly tell someone's purpose or motives. So, to have a successful relationship, close doors fully. Then, move forward!

Question:

Are you friends with an ex while you are in a new committed relationship? Is your new relationship worth the closure? Why or why not?

_____

_____

_____

_____

_____

_____

_____

_____

_____

_____

_____

_____

_____

_____

_____

Chapter 13

What is One Thing That Can Destroy a Relationship and Not Be Forgotten?

Ephesians 4:31-32

"Get rid of all bitterness, rage and anger, brawling and slander, along with every form of malice. Be kind and compassionate to one another, forgiving each other, just as in Christ God forgave you."

Everybody has different levels of tolerance. Some can't get over being lied to, cheated on, an outside child, abandonment, drug abuse, disrespect to their family out, or many other things. It's all in a person's tolerance and breaking point. The simple answer to the opening question would be "He's not the king God assigned for you." You could be the appetizer, main entrée, dessert, and the special gift set aside for a man. However, it would never be enough to a man that is simply not ready. That doesn't mean that his actions define your beauty.

It's been said that there's only one woman in a man's life that can make him change. For a while, I truly believed this was true. As I've gone through things, reevaluated situations, and gained wisdom, this is a false statement in my opinion. Let me further explain…
From birth, a man is introduced to a woman who is called his mother. In most cases, a mother or a mother figure has been involved with his early growth. She is changing, molding, and developing characteristics in him.

As the child enters child development such as daycare and school, he is introduced to female teachers who give him tools to enhance his education. He also meets other children of the opposite sex. That interaction sparks interest in what makes her different from him. If you ask a little boy if he is beautiful, most would respond "Girls are beautiful. Boys are handsome." They are taught early to find the beauty in a female.

Let's face it though. For those who have male figures, older brothers, and advanced friends, they instill the idea that there must be competition in how many women they can get, smash, or run crazy over them. I'm not sure why that is so cool in their minds. Still, men will encounter all types of women. Some women are reckless and simply lost. Some are confident in where they are in their lives. Although the women seem so different in comparison, the one thing they have in common is that they have gotten involved with a man that was simply not ready.

The men may even fall in love with the women, but because they have been so caught up with the impression of how many they must have, they simply mess up possibly great relationships. Some would even hurt a good relationship because they are so insecure by their guilt of what they've done in the past. They believe she will do it to them. Therefore, before he can get hurt, he will hurt her first.

During these breakups, he's developing mental lessons from it all. As he starts dating multiple women, he learns and changes something different for each. However, he doesn't make the full change until he's mastered the art of a relationship. He may not show his growth right away, but he learned something from the relationship - believe it or not. It hurts to know how much you invested into a man for him to be great for someone else. I'm sure I'm not the only one who thought that.

He may regret his actions, but pride will not allow him to show it. So, when that light bulb finally clicks, he then realizes what's important. His delayed commitment doesn't have anything to do with the women. It was the moment he was ready to be the man that God has called him to be. Then, he might be left hurt because he could be with the wrong woman when he finally decides to settle down.

Although you were hurt in the process of his growth, you should seek God's voice to see what lesson was gained from it as well. Even if that man is not the king God assigned for you, trust in God that the pain won't last always! You must fully recover so that you are strong enough for the next relationship. No one is perfect. The next guy will make mistakes of his own, and you need to be ready to endure what may come. If you didn't gain the lesson from the first relationship, you will find yourself attracted to a certain type who seems to have the same traits as the last.

It's not that he doesn't know you're beautiful. If he didn't find beauty in you, he wouldn't entertain you. Again, it's a pride thing! Beauty is beyond the physical surface. There will always be someone whose body seems more in place than yours. Their smile may be brighter or straighter. Their hair may be longer or more stylish, but we are all human. There are flaws in each of us, so the grass is never greener. It's only greener where you water it! Leave when you know it's toxic and they're just not who God has for you. Ladies, don't give up on yourself or love because of one bad relationship

I once made a huge mistake trying to force a relationship. I asked God to make him be the one I prayed for instead of trusting God to know who I am and to choose who's right for me. When we pray and ask God to remove those that are not of Him, we must be prepared because it may be people you least expect. As time progresses and the flesh and emotions weaken, we no longer have control over our feelings. A guy might have the image but lack the qualities that we specifically requested in prayer. We often think, *"Maybe my standards were set too high, and I could teach him."* NO! You know your worth, don't settle.

Ladies, we have something called intuition — one of our greatest attributes. We can sometimes see the mistake being planned. That's why we hurt more when a man lies. Through intuition, we already feel the truth. After a mistake has been made and you forgive, and this mistake is repeated, it is no longer a mistake. It is now a choice! If you decide to give another chance and his actions are repeated, his choices are now considered a habit. This repeated cycle is now toxic in your relationship.

If God has made it clear that he's not right for you, leave! If you choose not to obey God, you will suffer in silence, or God will make him leave you. When you force a man to stay, you are opening yourself up to accept whatever he brings to the table. You will not fully be happy if you are holding on to something that is for someone else. Save both of you a headache. The best advice I could give to you is to love yourself, so you won't be distracted by the wrong man's actions. If you allow certain behaviors, they will sell you dreams they cannot afford.

It's sad how emotional we are that we allow men to manipulate our mental, physical, emotional, and even spiritual growth. They allow us to fall so deep in love that we start to question our self-worth and beauty. He sees your beauty, but he notices it more when you are gone. He saw the strength that you would not settle, tolerate, or allow him to take advantage of you. He knows your worth and now has no choice but to respect it because you respect it. Once you move on and it's pure and not revenge, your happiness will shine without having to prove it to anyone. When your smile is big and bright, he then gets to see you in a different light.

Even if moving on means being single and free, work on yourself. Build on that business plan, new career, educational journey, or vision God placed on you. When you win at life, you are showing your ex that you didn't need them to get to the next level. However, you would have loved for them to be a part of your success. Philippians 4:13 says, "I can do all things through Christ who strengthens me." So, ladies, please remember this: You are beautiful, fearfully, and wonderfully made. Please never lose sight of that!

The biggest things that destroy the relationship after the problem occurred are pride and grudges. Some people are too prideful to admit their wrong or even apologize. Some are too hurt to accept apologies or even forgive. Certain situations feel like they're killing your self-esteem and confidence, but it's not over. It takes one opportunity to change your negative outlook on a painful situation. Take it! Forgiveness is not for their sanity. It's for your peace and happiness!

When you forgive someone, it doesn't mean you have to go back and deal with them. So even if you never receive that apology you know you deserve, just take that time to forgive! This is probably the most challenging but effective feat for me. After my hurt, I contemplated forgiveness for a while. I would type the words in a text and then delete it so many times. I wanted to say it, but I couldn't bring myself to send the words to him.

Nevertheless, I knew I needed to take that step to push myself to be a better me. I knew it would help me to let go of bitterness, anger, and pain.

To my past, I FORGIVE YOU! I forgive you for making me feel like "I" in a place where it should be "we." For kicking my soul until it turned dark… For pushing my mind to where I couldn't escape… For punching my heart until it shattered… For hurting my pride, emotions, and self-esteem. Although I didn't face physical abuse with you, I forgive you for verbally and emotionally abusing me to feel like nothingness in a place I only wished to be accepted. I forgive for allowing women to ride on the ship that was destined for only you and me to cross oceans. For humiliating me and giving women the power to laugh at me or assume I'm crazy, stupid, or a typical basic female while minimizing my worth of being a woman!

I forgive you for making me feel like I'm just like the females you often say are nothing... For making me feel year after year of disappointments of repeated mistakes that destroyed us. I forgive you for making me feel lonely in a world for two. For making me feel I wasn't enough… For going to bed at night without even touching me... For making me feel I don't exist in your world… For not coming home at night… For interfering with my trust… For putting the world before me and making me feel like the ugly duckling or witch's stepdaughter.

I forgive you for every social media account set up to betray me which led to you antagonizing my character. I forgive you for ignoring my pain and running or doing things to hurt me more if things didn't go your way. I forgive you for not professing your love and representing the love we were supposed to share… For not protecting me against family, friends, and even hidden enemies, I forgive you today for hurting me and allowing me to continue each day as low as can be.

I forgive you for expecting that I should trust again no matter what you did to me… For expecting me to come home no matter how empty the home is… For me trying not to act bothered no matter how much pain you made me feel… For telling me, "Let it go and never bring it up again," because you went to church and repented... For telling me, I better move at your speed or get lost… I forgive you for convincing me that I better forgive because Christ forgave… I forgive you for making me believe that I had better not leave no matter what the circumstances were because we agreed to love each other through everything.

I forgive you for using all of those sayings at some point in our relationship to manipulate me. I forgive you for putting me in a position to feel I have no escape if I want to respect God word. I forgive you for thinking you have taken my free will with torture. I forgive you for the pain you caused, and I pray to God that He eases my pain to overcome all negativity. I pray to God that He cleanses you purely and permanently. I thank God this was the biggest life lesson that changed me for the better. I will allow this moment to be the moment God uses me for a better purpose. I now can respectfully and purely say I forgive you and thank you because it gave me a source of strength I never knew I had!

Remember the three key elements for a successful relationship:

They are the 3 Cs: consistency, communication, and compromise.

Consistency

To be taken seriously, it's a must that you stay consistent. We repeat things that we don't fix! We often repeat steps in our lives because we haven't learned from the lesson in the first round. We get away with too much. It could be how we speed down a street without getting a ticket, so now we do it every day heading to work. You left work early and didn't get reprimanded, so you try it again every chance you get. You cursed your spouse out, and they didn't react, so you began to talk to them any ole way.

Getting away with things lead to habits... bad habits, that is! We often test the water without realizing there are a cause and effect. If we get away with our actions, we lose ourselves without caring what our actions may be doing to ourselves or others. Furthermore, we lose value in who we truly are. How many hearts have you broken? How many tears have you secretly cried or brought to someone's face? You brushed so much stuff under the rug or put on the persona that you are okay. Meanwhile, you are only killing yourself and who you worked hard to be by not dealing with the problems as they occur.

Society has made men believe that they can't be anything but strong without giving them the reality that they're human, too. Society has given ladies the idea that we must lose our value and hurt a man before he can hurt us. This way of thinking causes us to make poor choices and lose self-respect. On the positive note, when you are consistent with positive actions to match your words and heart, you can make the relationship remarkable.

Communication

Communication is my ultimate favorite element. From experience, it is truly the major key to a successful relationship or friendship. I believe that it is okay to walk away from situations that can cause you to change your character, but when things calm down, it is best to talk about what may have troubled you. Brushing things off without expressing your emotion can cause you self-anger, bitterness, and unsolved pain. A person cannot fix what they do not know, so do not be fearful to express what you feel even if they feel like you're talking too much. If they are unaware of the pain that their actions have caused you, they will often make the same mistakes without punishment because they never knew it affected, you.

Communication is a ticket out of so many things we encounter. Someone once asked me, "What if you do communicate and they don't seem to listen?" If a person can go to sleep peacefully with their actions knowing they have hurt you, they are simply defining their character before you. If they can't look you in your eyes and feel the depths of your soul from your pain, there is a lack of connection between the two of you. Please understand that if an argument is heated, they are not in the position to understand you. This is solely for when things have calmed down.

If they are not willing to resolve the issue to make the relationship work, there will be a lot of buried pain developing in the future. It is your choice to keep that person around. In most cases, their actions show how careless they are about you and how selfish they can be. They might even become complacent in your life believing they can never be replaced. Again, they only created habit because they always get away with it. Bad habits like lacking communication can also lead to trust issues and doubts. If you are the one who lacks communication, there are ways to work on that.

Compromise

It is very important to compromise with your significant other. I strongly believe when you love someone, the smile on their face truly fulfills the happiness within yourself. It is okay to step outside of your comfort zone to make sure they remain happy. When they're happy, they will bring you happiness as well. Ladies, if he wants to watch the game only on Monday, but your favorite show comes on that same day, compromise with him! Learn the game or cook and clean for him. You can watch your show later via on-demand or on a re-run.

Fellas, I'm not letting you off that easy. You know women have long days at work and coworkers have ticked her off. You may not always like hearing her talk about her problems because it feels like you are gossiping, but just listen and show support! Sometimes, go the extra mile and give her advice. Just knowing her man has her back means everything. Making this sacrifice is amazing. However, it is your job never to lose sight of your standards and self-worth. You are not a joke and should not be mistaken for one. You gained too much wisdom along the way to be a fool or a dummy just to have someone in your life. That goes for family, friends, associates, and your spouse.

When they are not treating you with respect, this is not a moment to compromise yourself. If someone wants to leave your side, let them leave. If they find others more appealing to their desires, accept what is and move on with your life. Tell yourself, "I'm in control of my fate. I will not settle for less than I deserve. I will not beg for anyone's attention or time. I'm one of a kind and not duplicated. Anyone that has me in their life is blessed, so I refuse to believe less of me as if I am nothing." That's not being arrogant but understanding that God created you in His light. Don't allow anyone to dim it. God said it best in Psalm139:13-14, "For you created my inmost being; you knit me together in my mother's womb. I praise you because I am fearfully and wonderfully made. Your works are wonderful."

Applying these three key elements in your life will allow healthier relationships to prosper. I know when we read different things, we always think about that person in our life that can use this information. Perfect! I also want you to take time to evaluate yourself to improve the skills you may fall short on. It never takes too much for us to just improve some things within us. There are so many other qualities that can help build and develop a great loving relationship. Go into the relationship with a positive mind and remember that you fail when you do not try. If you make an effort, learn from it, and push through, then you have succeeded!

I never felt so free in my life until I took back what the devil tried to steal from me. That was my peace, happiness, self-esteem, confidence, and smile. I was once a victim of depression, mental abuse, and emotional abuse. I allowed negative actions to destroy me. I believed many women were better than me. Furthermore, I allowed myself to feel I wasn't enough, and that was my biggest mistake.

Ladies, patience is not only referring to a man being able to hold your purse as you try on the twelfth outfit for the second time in a mall. Fellas, it's also not just the time a woman has to sit at your homeboy's house as you shout for the game. In the beginning, all those things will happen. Know that patience is understanding that you are bringing two individuals together that come from different backgrounds. Things will not always be smooth sailing. When the times get rough, you shouldn't be so quick to give up. Instead, pray and ask God to help order your steps.

When the Bible speaks of kindness, I strongly believe that's self-explanatory. You should never compete with your spouse. The goal is to share dreams and visions and conquer each one together. It's okay to share God's blessings and give recognition. However, boasting as if the two of you made it big on your own will surely have you knocked off your high horse. Growing into your own comes with work. It's the man's job to protect every ounce of your body, but he's also supposed to protect your heart. This will help with gaining trust.

Question:

Who or what caused you pain that you still harbor? You too, should write out your forgiveness.

_____

_____

_____

_____

_____

Final Words of Encouragement
from Toni Dyson

Young women suffer from situations like this daily. No problem is too big or too small for God to heal. If you are challenged with depression, please understand that you are not alone. It is okay to reach out for help. Family and friends are not always as understanding as you may need them to be. They may cause you more pain than you experienced before you reached out to them. I can't promise that they will not judge or gossip about you, but I can say try your very best to seek professional help to direct you on a positive and productive path. Don't run from your problems. Trust the process!

Prayer:

Lord, I come to you right now saying thank you. Thank you for allowing your message to be used through me. Thank you for placing all the right people in my life to help me along this journey. Writing a book is not easy, but when you said to do it, you made a way. Lord, I come to you saying thank you for the readers who prayerfully got something from this book other than "another story." I am praying that you reach down and heal whatever situation they may battle. Bind up the depression, suicidal thoughts, anger, jealousy, and envious thoughts the enemy is planting within. Release generational curses. Protect all. Bless all. In Jesus' name, Amen!

www.ingramcontent.com/pod-product-compliance
Lightning Source LLC
Chambersburg PA
CBHW020843260626
47169CB00003B/1110